Hvala,

Franek

The Philosopher's Walk,
Tooth Bus
&
A Mouthful Of China

F. J. NANIĆ

to read
Death + the Dervish — p. 73

Knowledge does not travel but it is traveled to.

Malik ibn Anas

As the non-threatening professor had walked so quietly through the streets of Königsberg, none who saw him had suspected that his mind was filled with the sparks and crackles of ideas which would develop an explosive power sufficient to propel the world into a new age.

Paul A. Schons

What's remembered perishes, what's written remains...

Basheskia

CONTENTS

FROM JACK'S MANUAL

F. J. NANIĆ

TOOTH BUS

One day you wake up tormented by missed opportunities.

Literally at the end of the western world, just an hour's drive east of the Pacific Ocean, you start questioning the pros and cons of it all, tossing and turning in bed like a fish out of water.

Weigh it up, my father would say, *put it on the scales and see which side tips over…*

A number of years already, I've been weighing different reasons up and down. The only thing I achieved is to find myself in the middle of the scales with my arms stretched out as if I were a petrified *Justitia.*

I can't move left or right.

Still I am moving *on* already late for an appointment, going to catch a dental bus. Courtesy of *All Saints Church,* 41st and Woodstock.

I am scheduled for 8.45, *if they manage to work me in,* as I was told on the phone.

I had been redialing them for half an hour straight, hearing that sweet voicemail every minute, telling me to *dial 911 in case it's an emergency.*

And now I'm smack bang in the middle of the church, *All Saints*

3

(I asked them for a blank sheet of paper to write this down), surrounded by misfits with no insurance, unable to pay.

It's the same hall we were sitting in fifteen years ago, refugees from Bosnia in a Russian Church, facing Vladivostok somewhere across the Pacific Ocean. Ready to start from scratch, confused by our high hopes, survival instincts, and hairy past. Looking forward, trying to envision some better days ahead.

Fifteen years after, I'm catching a dental bus that comes once a month to help only if you're in pain or have a broken tooth.

I have neither, a filling came out. I'm just sitting here trying to grasp it all while at the same time a Vietnam Veteran across the table is telling his life story to a retired receptionist.

He's been *happily* married for fifty-three years, *still not knowing his wife's favorite color.*

His bright red cap displayed *3d Marine Division* in big yellow letters.

His attitude was similar to my father's and I couldn't help believing that somehow through that old fellow he was there watching over me.

He kept going on about one of his aunts that never left Oklahoma City.

Her only wish was to see the ocean, and as they took her there, just before seeing it, one could hear the waves roaring and tumbling in the distance.

What's that noise?

They tried to calm her down saying:

It's the ocean, don't worry, it's why we came here for!

But, no sir, no way she was going to move an inch forward.

All she wanted then was to go back to her Oklahoma City…

The next thing he talked about was his wonderful grandkids…

It's more fun having grandkids than kids, that's for sure!

Maybe because he could play with them and, while doing chores, *they could have had as many breaks as they wanted, and then go across the street to Danny's…*

He went about how fantastic his childhood was:

They were not rich, but never hungry!

They'd polish their plates off, and the only thing he didn't like was *spinach.*

His brother disliked *carrots…*

The other day one of his grandsons came back from Afghanistan and telephoned him, *just to let him know he's crossed the pond…*

Two chairs down a black guy was sitting overwhelmed by his *SMART* phone, and at the next table a couple of overweight women with their thighs the size of a telephone pole each. Half of their teeth were missing inside their hefty heads, their hoarse voices broken by a smoker's cough.

The receptionist was the only one acting *normal,* even kinder than *that*, almost as if appointed by God Almighty, or one of his archangels.

She made sure we had enough pencils, paper, and magazines to read, trying to lighten up the *situation.*

After forty years in a truck company I ended up with fifty pens in my bag!

She said that laughing after I returned the one I borrowed.

American jokes were not rubbing off on me. I just smiled as if I'd listen to children that tried to get away caught stealing cookies from a jar and then scared making fun of it.

A few Russian ladies came in and greeted her, heading toward different doors.

Given away by their accents, they couldn't hide the fact that their attire made them looking American or European on the surface only. It seemed that no one else but them really cared.

In Russia, like back home, one was deprived of the western consumer trappings for too long. People watched too much TV and imagined everything was *peachy keen* over here. Some of them managed balancing out their attitude and expectations as long as they were able to wear their favorite brands, driving around in their favorite cars.

Sitting there with *Death and the Dervish* on the table, I worried about lying that I felt pain.

I encircled *YES* convincing myself I would explain it once I was admitted. I kept reading the book trying to ignore my whereabouts.

I overheard one of those obese women praising Google for helping her with her kids' homework.

The other one didn't know when was the last time she saw a dentist, so she asked someone on the phone.

Then the male nurse came in for the next two patients.

He looked like a shorter and older version of my friend Robert. The receptionist kept it all on the bright side, but he was the total opposite. Regimental, protestant, and dead serious about his purpose on Earth. The world was somewhere in the middle of the scales, between him and the kind receptionist.

The black guy and I were called up and we followed him through the church to the back door. The windows were stained blue and there was enough homely light inside, as opposed to the catholic cathedrals I knew in Europe. One of the Russian ladies walked between the aisles in a pair of tight blue jeans with a bag full of groceries.

The bus door opened and we got in, the black guy to the left, and me to the right.

You can sit in the recliner, the male nurse pointed out politely and went on with his business.

I sat there waiting with *Death and the Dervish* on my lap.

The doctor showed up and looked at me cautiously, I guess because of all the different walks of life that walk in to his traveling ordination.

What can we do for you?

It's a well-known question one hears a lot, but the answer to it is never clear. I pointed to my lower jaw and showed him *the* tooth.

It hurts a bit, I said a bit embarrassed that I had to lie in order to have anything done.

How long has it been hurting you?

About two weeks, I said trying to sound nonchalant about it, as though I had other more important problems.

He probed it with his sharp tools and tried to move it left and right with his fingers.

I feigned a little nervousness but didn't want it to seem too painful. Because then he might have suggested pulling it out. I was very diplomatic about it, as if I talked about a loose button on my shirt.

It seems like we have a root canal problem here. We can either pull it out or put a filling in, but it might cause a reaction and swelling later...

I was taken aback that he even considered a possibility of putting a filling in, and I stuck with it.

I'd really like to save it, I said, and if something goes wrong later, I can always pull it out...

It's what I would do if I were you!

Always, always, always, the same old *seeming quandary,* and I still didn't get used to it.

They already know the answer, but they wait and see if you'd come up with it as well.

Back home, it's what you'd expect from a doctor—to give you the options and guide you through it. Here, they give you the options, but you are to guide yourself, through thick and thin. A limited liability issue. No risks undertaken on their part.

Well, then, let's get started with numbing you a bit…

As he fiddled with instruments, I was truly nervous about the overall hygiene, considering that only the bottom rung of society frequented this kind of facilities. I knew I was going to immediately take off my jeans and sweater and do the laundry when I get back home. But I couldn't wash the poke of a needle once it gets under my skin.

You don't really need to numb me, I told him trying to sound indifferent.

Oh, I don't think you'd like that…

Well, I guess I'm a bit nervous about the needles and how sterile they are…

He seemed to have appreciated my bringing it up and told me not to worry:

We only use them once here…

But he also reminisced a bit, as if sharing one of his private secrets with me:

Oh, boy, when I was volunteering in Honduras, they would just wipe down the same needle and use it all over again… They didn't even sharpen it up… One could see something living inside… Poor kids…

I was truly amazed about what people would share once you pushed the right buttons, intentionally or not. I was also amazed that my fear somewhere else would be legitimate.

So, they *do* use the same needle after they just *wipe it down…*

I thought only junkies would get on with it.

You just wave your hand if it hurts. Pretty soon you'll have the sensation of a fat lip…

I nodded still in disbelief I was going to actually save a tooth for free. I looked through the big windshield, the sun was shining outside, first autumn leaves drifting by. Again I remembered the line from a movie I saw a weak ago:

Kindness makes time go off its course and turns it into eternity.

It's exactly how it felt. The time stood still. As if I traveled on a magic bus. We had just pulled over so that they can fix my tooth, and then we moved on, kindness is all we needed to stop *Time* and just worry about *Space,* enough room for everybody…

They woke me up from my daydreaming ready to work.

I asked about the X-ray, and he was a bit surprised that he forgot to even look at it. For the first time his face loosened up into a smile that looked like a faint chance of it.

The root canal has already been done—you're lucky!

He gave me a friendly pat on the shoulder and started drilling.

I truly *was* lucky. But I couldn't even remember when that root canal was done.

It took me back to my previous thinking about the last fifteen years as if they were gone by in a flash before a dying man's eyes. One said *make sure it's worth watching,* as if the most of it had happened to someone else. I couldn't even remember I had a root canal done. I surely would have felt *that.*

I remembered other *root canals* though, done right through my heart…

Meanwhile, the dentist and his nurse exchanged their vacation stories. They both liked Alaska and Victoria, BC.

There is a ferry from Port Angeles around 5 p.m., if you don't want to go via

San Juan, said the nurse while *curing* my new filling. It was accomplished by shining a blue light on it.

There you go, it's all done!

The dentist announced that *Time* was up and running again. I used the opportunity to ask him about the *danger* of mercury fillings, since I carried quiet a few in my mouth over a few decades.

If anyone should get poisoned by it, it's the dentists, and I haven't heard of any such cases...

I was not going to push my luck mentioning what I'd found on the Internet about *dental amalgam leaching mercury vapor into the mouth and brain.*

It is approved as safe when it shows up in our urine, but it causes damage to plumbing pipes.

To avoid their licenses being revoked, dentists stick with what their dental associations stand for.

Originating from the old world, I was full of it. A third of my teeth were already filled with mercury. But today a tooth was saved thanks to *All Saints* and a merciful dentist, and I surely was grateful!

Praise the Lord!

NAVIGATING THE SYSTEM

I woke up way past the early hours of this *Black Friday* morning.

Last night I went to bed after midnight desperately trying to establish a platform for my books online.

It was kind of a pre-Black Friday deal.

Unbelievable, how many tactful writers soared out there with their *I-want-to-lick-it* book covers. It reminded me of what Jimmy Page said once:

Thank God they don't teach rock guitar at school…

Well, if I wanted to be noticed among two million authors, I was to solicit honest reviews, doing it like some kind of a womanizer, with my hand between their legs, talking about religion or new amendments.

A *Starbuck* girl yesterday asked me:

Are you over fifty-five?

I laughed in disbelief. She was going to give me a senior discount.

Just a few months ago I was still thirty-eight or forty-three max.

I got used to it so much I wouldn't give it a time of day. But when I heard *over fifty-five,* it made my *old* flesh crawl. I went back to

Evelyn, with my fifty cents *dearer* drip coffee, and said:

This is what happens to me when I hang out with you…

We both laughed and continued translating historical events that occurred almost two hundred years ago. It made us feel forever young—not that we had time to think about it. We were getting behind.

The Bosnian uprising was about twenty pages ahead of us and we still didn't find a publisher willing to *wheel and deal* it. Moreover, our author, in his late eighties, could have died on us any time, and then we'd be left with a satisfaction that at least we didn't have to translate anything *shape shifting* and *paranormal.*

History was still right there where one left it, turned over a few times as a medium steak well done. Around us new generations looked like half-successful abortions. They wouldn't have a clue what we were rambling about. Nothing in their eyes showed for it. From the core of their hearts sprouted extended baby needs' checklists, and one was rather puzzled what to do about them, particularly if a regular breastfeeding was out of the question.

But let's get back to this *Black Friday* morning…

I got up after eight realizing I didn't have enough money to look for any deals, so I continued working on my *platform* until the phone rang.

They needed me in the *Keiser* E.R. as soon as possible.

It's nice to be needed, *tous les temps en temps.* But I was still in my PJ's just digesting a teaspoon of chia seed in a glass of water, waiting for that first drip coffee to hit the roof of my mouth.

I didn't even get a chance to read the morning paper that we don't receive. *I worked on my own damn paper.*

It didn't really matter, as long as thoughts kept being generated and the paper was used with a continuous printer, in perpetual fan folding.

En fin, bref!

I use some French here since I interpreted in French.

It happened only once, when a little girl from around Bordeaux had to have her tonsils removed.

She was really sweet as her nature coincided with her demeanor. For a while she made me feel as if I were somewhere in France. The blonde doctor would occasionally interrupt it with her ducky comments casting bewildered looks in my direction.

This morning I recalled it with a smile, driving through the cold *Black Friday* rain on my way to Clackamas. It's where all the outlets were. It's where the Keiser Medical Center was.

I wondered what part of France would my next patient be from.

It happened every once in a blue moon that I was to speak the language. It felt a bit awkward. There was nothing French around here except for the untraceable tracks of fur trappers from a time long gone, when they came here among the first non-Indians, trading in uncharted territory *pro pelle cutem.*

It was the Latin motto on the *HBC* coat of arms, meaning: *a skin for a skin.*

It is all history now, Radisson and des Groseilliers *n'y sont plus disponible.*

I was on my way to interpret for Guillaume.

It was a bit ironic. A Bosnian and a French meeting near the Oregon Trail End Point.

After the usual bleak and beige petrified plasticity of the medical center—where they first greet me as a potential patient, and then smile with their eyes upon my introduction—I was given the well known left-right directions through the off-white corridors.

The last time in the E.R. we waited for almost eight hours. Procedures, procedures…

It is enough to put one off it for a whole year, seeing different

13

cases as knackered as horses that can no longer work.

FYI, a *knackery* is different from a *slaughterhouse,* where animals are killed for human consumption. When they are *ready for the knacker's yard,* old horses are made into glue and dog food…

In the room *C/15* no French little girls waited with sore throats.

There was a skinny man lying and shaking like a leaf.

His smile, his face, his whole head seemed attached to his body, as if having nothing to do with it. His eyes were gray and foggy contrasting his pearly whites each time he opened his wide mouth to say something or just smile like an innocent boy. His tongue seemed like a bright pink little creature living independently in his mouth. It had way less pigmentation than an average white man tongue.

Guillome was from Africa, Nigeria. He's been an *akata* for five years now.

It's not derogatory.

It means *a cat that doesn't live at home like a wild non-domesticated cat.*

He reminded me a bit of a shy Cosby.

A Cosby that never made it to TV, becoming a janitor instead.

His wife too.

She sat in the corner munching on something with that peaceful gaze of a friendly camel.

It is not derogatory either. There was certain peace about them that felt awkward, as if an African oasis were contained within a plastic cube.

Outside was gray and clammy.

As far as one could see, a big gray woolen sky stretched over the blocks of various buildings and roads between them filled with ever moving cars. One instinctively ran indoors to hide from it. Once inside, one was to face the music of an almost virtual reality.

Guillome was real all right.

Dark chocolate dark, he stood out even more stretched out horizontally in an off-white surrounding. His teeth were whiter than mine could ever be. He smiled like *Kunta Kinte* just unchained off the *Roots*, finally free. But *something* was shaking inside.

What's shaking?

I could hear it resonating inside my head.

Instead, I was to use a professional greeting with a polite:

What brought you here today?

It was *simple*. Fatigue, tremors, vomiting, not being able to eat, feeling weak...

The nurse came in and said there was a problem with his kidneys.

She did it in a flight attendant manner. Probably happy to have a job providing enough means to support her dream. People like her make one feel good about America, as if it were a place to be.

In Europe one would definitely encounter some frowning here and there. But not here, sir. *The show must go on.* The only dent in is that it seems *too relaxing*.

Funny, if you try to Google it, it comes up only with *to* or *how to relax?*

Apparently, too much of it doesn't exist. It's what people are not prepared for, but indirectly are trained to expect or provide it. A good service. At least here.

Mind you, in Turkey too.

Or wherever people have based their expectations upon the mountain of money they want to make.

But we drifted off the subject now...

Kidneys, *eh?*

It reminded me of my kidney stones and a *giving birth experience*. To produce and deliver a 3 mm stone, one is to feel like dying for about a week, doubled over with pain, almost unable *to go*.

After my first attack—I was in a pub having a beer, of a sudden winding up in the toilet busting to pee, throbbing like an overblown balloon, solid under pressure—my neighbor Jeff helped me to his car and took me to a Milwaukee hospital. I was doubled like a folding chair.

The nurse shrugged it off with:

You should have had another beer...

It took my mind off pain. I had already had a couple and I thought one more would have made me explode. Sometimes you are to *keep going through hell till you get out.* In any case, they gave me morphine to relieve pain until my fingernails went blue.

I didn't tell all that to Guillome. I just said his nausea might be connected with a kidney stone. That was another trap.

How to say a *kidney stone* in French?

I knew *pierre* meant stone, and kidneys were something starting with R. *Renal?*

It was embarrassing enough.

I was summoned as a *French Medical Interpreter,* otherwise Guillome could have gotten by with his patois and his broken English. I was to act quickly so I threw *les problems renals* in the air like juggling balls. My luck referred to the fact that Guillome came from a former English colony, but went to a French school, and with his wife he used Kanuri.

I could have pretty much said anything without preventing crossover between the French and Latin and it would have sounded *medical* enough. Of course, it would be ignoble and I wasn't that far off with *les problems renals.*

The better way would be "les problemes rénaux," *quand meme.*

The proper way is *Calculs rénaux.* But I'm afraid Guillome's French wasn't advanced enough to understand it.

His wife Rita looked at me as if I said something out of the Bible.

She couldn't read.

She spoke a version of Kanuri-English imbued with half-eaten words that she pushed around her mouth together with food, at times thrusting her tongue in her cheek.

(While I'm writing this, in a *Starbucks* in Sellwood, a few tables down, a myopic teenage girl is sucking on her thumb, while the radio plays *Something's gotta hold on me*.)

Rita was my savior. Every time she opened her mouth, she grabbed everybody's attention. We'd all look at her enchanted by that half-eaten language that matched her snoozy eyes, as if she were a bird at the outer edge of a flock at roost, having both eyes half-open instead of just one.

One couldn't tell if she was truly half-asleep, and if one of her brain hemispheres snoozed as the other remained awake and alert. Both her eyes were half-open and vigilant making sure the birds *in the middle of the flock* are fully resting, sleeping with both eyes closed.

After I exhausted my kidney-stone narrative together with due politeness and formalities, the only thing left was to wait.

E.R. was like a purgatory.

I used to spend there many days and nights with my father and his cancer.

Now that he was gone, as if it became some kind of a tradition, I continued helping other patients. It was pretty much the only work available. There was not much of it, and it eventuated occasionally as other people did their full eight-hour and overtime shifts.

By nature interested in making more money, consequently they wound up being the most frequent patients, suffering from backache, hemorrhoids, acid reflux, diabetes, and all that jazz.

Last time in the E.R. I waited with a colonoscopy patient for about six hours just to be admitted. Another fifty minutes followed in a room full of instruments, computers, additional four stuff members, myself, and a patient lying sideways numbed to sleep, as they pumped some air up the colon to *open it* first.

Needless to mention its natural reaction blowing the air back…

A curious thing happened now…

As I Googled about *blowing the air back,* I came across *blow her back out:* "when you do it doggy-style, causing her ass cheeks to clap together and she can't walk the next day or two," and *lower back blow out:* "the other day I was sitting in a chair bent over assembling a night stand that I bought at Ikea; when I stood up my lower back locked up."

One below the other, very interesting…

No cheeks clapping here though, with six people in an almost airtight room.

Just a stale, colon air blowing back, as we watched a little camera going *up* the tubes courtesy of the latest technology.

Four staff members performed their ethical duties at the same time reminiscing about *Dancing With The Stars* from the night before.

What was my role there apart from inhaling a stale colon air, I stopped trying to fathom.

I just became a part of the landscape, a piece of furniture amazed by the way everything functioned. I was there to also ensure that verbal communications between the patient and doctors functioned properly, but since the patient was sound asleep, there was nothing else for me but to wait for her awakening.

Back in the room with Guillome and his wife Rita, we still waited.

The nurse popped in and out a few times thanking us kindly for being patient. It was a bit unusual for a busy E.R.

I didn't mind since I had D.H. Lawrence's *Apocalypse* in my backpack, and the time was ripe to continue reading it. I brought it with me, as I was not being able to put it down. I was moved by its imponderable value. It was published 1931 and it said this:

In democracy, bullying definitely takes the place of power. The modern

Christian state is a soul-destroying force, for it is made up of fragments which have no organic whole, only a collective whole.

It struck me sounding familiar, as if he talked about collective socialism vs. individualism, but then again he openly argued that:

No man is or can be a pure individual. The mass of men have only the tiniest touch of individuality: if any. The mass of men live and move, think and feel collectively, and have practically no individual emotions, feelings or thought at all. They are fragments of collective and social consciousness. It has always been so. And will always be so.

It's when the doctor rushed in apologizing for taking so long and immediately adding:

How long have you had AIDS?

I just couldn't believe my ears. It had crossed my mind seeing twiggy Guillome shaking like a leaf. But since nobody mentioned it, I focused on *kidneys*.

Why didn't they warn me upfront? They could have said:

You are to interpret for an AIDS patient—*are you okay with that?*

Just to prepare myself better and be careful, if nothing else…

But there was no time to mull over it. I was to do my job, although Guillome understood the questions quiet well.

Was it transmitted through a sexual contact?

The whites of his eyes were whiter than the walls around us. The gray in them was blurry. He hadn't eaten for days. He stopped smiling too. No, it wasn't sexually transmitted.

Was it transmitted during drug use?

He was a bit uncomfortable looking down and saying it was through blood transfusion back in Africa.

The doctor didn't seem convinced, but she also didn't have time to mull over it:

Your kidneys have shut down…and our kidney specialists are on their way to talk to you…

How in the world he could still smile and be so calm?

It was the first time in my life I faced such unlikely situation.

One specialist came in first and she—spoke French. An intermediate level.

Of course, they are all so nice and kind to Guillome and Rita that I couldn't help wondering whether it was because of AIDS or because they were from Africa. Or both.

Again, no time for ruminating over it. I had to be very careful about the doctor's tentative French. Every time she didn't know the right word, standing astride like a cowgirl, she'd look at me over her shoulder as if I was to pour another champagne.

When it came down to how to say *kidney function,* she was quiet surprised it was something she knew already—*fonction renale.* Physiology parlance.

I kept praising her for it meant less work for me. Why not let her show off a bit? It was like a group therapy combining psychology, immunology, and lexicology.

Guillome kept smiling, Rita kept munching on something, and the doctor practiced her French, retaining what she had learned and developing fluency. Her accent was almost lost.

The party started when the other kidney specialist arrived.

She looked like an Asian Simpsons' version with her bulgy eyes and stick figure. She was there to confirm Guillome's *renal failure,* as he kept smiling like an African guru. She bulged her eyes a bit more, carefully announcing a solution:

You could start dialysis…

Now Guillome almost laughed.

How am I going to work?

His wife Rita swallowed a morsel before grinning.

The specialists first looked at each other in disbelief, then at me.

Guillome had said it in English, so I just shrugged it off smiling as if I was renewing my driver's license. They have probably never heard it before. Neither have I.

A guy with failed kidneys is worried more about his job then about his life.

But to live you need money, and for that you have to work…

Rita nodded proudly supporting her husband's wisdom.

She said something no one understood. It was irrelevant and the doctors kept working on their ethical part.

It was the same old passive-aggressive *sometimes we win and you lose* style trying to lead into a win-win outcome.

Guillome should have been awarded an Oscar for his role. Just by calmly accepting his misfortune he got Fate generously smiling upon him.

He knew how to talk to the ladies too. He was subservient to a point, knowing when to back off and let his calm and proud silence rule.

The two specialists practically started almost singing while begging with their little voices, as they'd encountered a man that peacefully put a janitor job over his failed kidneys.

He wisely and indirectly plastered them on their own turf.

And he wasn't alone. His wife backed him up. Now a whole team of people listened to her trying to, *with all due respect,* distinguish her half-eaten words from half-eaten food.

It was all about a nifty health insurance game modeled after the ancient rules of functioning that walk you through *your* life at different stages and let you choose if you want to proceed with or without it.

For each consideration, you get an explanation of how you and your happiness will turn out, up or down. The whole thing is charming and does a great job of putting askew concepts into a context that makes sense for everyone: who controls state government, and who controls whom in general.

Guillome put it in a nutshell choosing work over life. Because he knew a simple truth. One cannot work dead. To keep you alive they need to push the right buttons and make their little game work.

It's not *men in black* that control everything. It's *women in white*. But silence was not giving consent in this case. Guillome was to sign that he accepted dialysis, and they were to arrange the whole thing work. Had he not signed, the whole system would collapse *ethically*.

What would be the point of the whole hullabaloo if it didn't work in the end? All those machines and instruments and doctors and nurses and social workers and receptionists and cleaners…

One man could have abolished it by just not giving his consent, and then the news would go something like:

An African refugee died due to AIDS and kidney failure not being able to cover the expenses.

Those two specialists in white cloaks would loose their meaning. The whole health system would become a joke. Therefore they kept persisting, requesting me to translate word for word, while Guillome kept grinning calmly choosing work over life, beating them at their own game, worried about dialysis interfering with his shifts. Because his boss needed *someone*, and he could be easily replaced.

The doctors understood all that, but in order to do anything he needed to live first:

Don't worry about it, just do your dialysis! We can navigate the system better than you…

Guillome was either a plain innocent African angel, or he learned his lesson well after contracting AIDS, escaping his restless country, and working five years as a janitor, taking care of buildings, making sure they functioned properly so that people could use their facilities at need.

Brian Weiss was right about the patient-doctor dynamics:

They paid the bills, flattered me, made me feel indispensable to them, and reinforced the stereotype of the physician as demigod in our society.

It also stemmed from the fact that doctors were God's little helpers, because if *everything is in God's hands* and *everything comes from God,* here on Earth they are his hands, at least one of them.

GOD ALMIGHTY

No matter how many forms a belief takes, first set the record straight unless you don't mind it skipping...

Let's say, if we believed that *Goddess* was in charge, since we can *believe whatever we want,* then we'd be surrounded by *Unconditional Love* that we *normally* get from our mothers.

But if our God is *Our Father,* then we're in it for paternal *Conditional Love,* and thus our God is jealous.

There are no missed opportunities.

It's what we imagine. *If we believe in it,* they all come from our *Creator,* and since his love is conditional, he only wants to see how much of it is there for him.

He wants to be loved *first* and *foremost.* And if you, *God forbid,* forget about *Him* even for a second, carried away by the opportunities that *He* had sent your way, well, then imagine a *CEO* you work for and pass by in a hurry because you have some important errands to run...

Okay, maybe your *CEO* won't recognize you, then how about your *Boss?*

Our *Dear God* gives us everything and takes it back in due time.

There is nothing, *absolutely nothing,* we can bring with us on our last journey.

Not even the loves of our lives, or our precious children.

Deceased family members might be waiting for us up there, as it's where we all meet *eventually*. But in the meantime, our soul is to travel stripped naked and alone.

It's to happen even if our God is *It*.

Neither maternal nor paternal—maybe *pediatric?*

What if our God was a humongous child playing in a cosmological bathtub, squeezing starry duckies?

Just kidding! I only say it because we say *it* for a child, but *it* could be anything!

A sophisticated hydra, or…shall we say *Love*.

Is God Love?

Or, let's put it this way:

Has Love ever left you gutted?

When and *if*—it always *leaves* you gutted, unless your patches have patches…

That means your soul is *so* patched up that by then your guts are gone together with the glory.

You don't need them anymore.

You discover your third eye and realize it has a bird's perspective. It's *elevated*.

With your guts gone, your mind is out of the gutter.

It's like a hysterectomy of your *glorious guts*. You can see it all clearly from an equal distance. Love, Hope, Faith, Truth, Beauty, Freedom…

And there goes your *Nirvana*.

There is your *Satori*.

With a perspective as though you were a bird, *or God*, down there you can see how, as if high on clean mountain air, *Love* walks on a rope tied between *Faith* and *Hope*. A rope at times loose, depending on the firmness of both sides.

Hope is the worst of evils, for it prolongs the torments of men, said Nietzsche.

For that to blame is more those who *give* crumbs of it as if feeding pigeons that peck like robots. It's equal to crumbling into pebbles a rock of punishment above someone's head.

Apparently, they feed them until they're symbolically grown into white doves of peace. Which only becomes a metaphorical gavage-based break between wars. There is no lasting *Peace* without *Love*.

Love helps *Hope* and *Faith* to become one that in the end it resembles, if you wish, *Holy Trinity*. But it only resembles it, since the real one consists of Love, Freedom, and Truth, independent from one another, while *Hope, Faith, and Love* mutually support each other so that all three of them could survive.

Freedom doesn't need *Hope,* and *Faith* either. The same goes with *Truth*. They exist of their own accord. One beautiful, the other sharp, and *Love* is strong as long as *Hope* and *Faith* are mutually inclusive.

Indeed, *Love* sprouts out of the purity of an emotion inspired by beauty, which again is impossible without genuine goodness and freedom of a person to feel anything.

After that come *Hope* and *Faith* in the eternity of an enchanting moment. One wants it to last, while it exists only in the present, which ticks steady as long as we're totally aware of it.

Thus, it never leaves you.

You feel gutted because your guts were full of glory. Once you lose it, it feels as though losing a *bad attitude*.

Then you realize your *Love* is always with you, *within*, like God.

Since it's not material, you can't touch it and, most of all, *you can't own it.*

Otherwise, it's a holistic experience yours to keep forever.

GARDEN OF OSCAR

The garden-story described in the *Book of Genesis* is surrounded by unreliable facts about the meaning of the word *Eden* and whether the garden was in the east of it, or Eden itself was in the east...

Those are rather geographical and lexical than metaphysical issues.

Qur'an has a *slightly* different approach and it is mainly regarding the abstract meaning of the word *garden*.

One indeed is strictly dependable on its translation and authentic interpretation.

I was blessed by a 1969 edition that is rich with explanations not to be found elsewhere like:

Paradise, according to Qur'an, is a garden arranged by one's own work and effort.

Those who enter Paradise, as they start enjoying its fruits, will say:

"Indeed they are the same as we were given before," for it will be the first fruit of their own work that they'll enjoy.

In other words, whatever one did down on Earth, however he tended his *garden,* or better said: However one lived his life, the reflection of it will be displayed on a big, eternal screen of which he'll be the part of.

Johnstone film

So, maybe you're not going to partake in creating a Hollywood blockbuster pay-per-view special event. But you'll definitely be the director of your own pay-as-you-go *eternal* version.

Weigh it up, and think about which one is more important.

What an Academy Award you'll be given, and whose uncle does it remind you of?

In a wild combination, one should call it *Garden of Oscar...*

AN EASY READ

All our moving around was *preparations for leaving the building*.

It's done in life-size phases:

Conceiving a life, coming to life, bringing to life, using life sculptures, relating to animate existence, continuing for a lifetime, never really sure about *the* source of vitality...

At times it is *She,* as we look at her enchanted in awe. It could be our daughter, but it could be anyone's—*a God's creation?*

She actually exists as a subject for an artist, *painted from life,* now uncannily animated. She even led a hard life, sometimes running for it, as if it were a presidency of some sort.

One planned on an attempt to live a more sustainable lifestyle with the little help of our dear technology, knowing we wouldn't be able to afford it. But we pitched it at exactly the right angle to get all the possible sunshine and make it feel relatively painless.

And then *she* walked in, sweeping us of our feet.

The key part of the roof!

Eaves and walls are easily accessible, what else do we need?

It's a pure application of all we know so far, and it's just standing there, in the foyer, someone better take her coat, offer her a drink...

It turns out she's there as *our* refreshment, a sight for our sore eyes overstrained from staring at big pictures. It's why we did it in the first place, trying to avoid all the eyesores from smaller paintings that were just plain ugly.

So, you want beauty, eh?

There it is, now sustain it!

Make it last, avoiding a line of sight propagation!

You are to make sure not to cross the lines of flight of all those steady yellow jackets.

They are not your honeybees.

They just *sting ya* and *sting ya* until you swell up like a fat balloon.

Hence, she puts our minds at ease at first sight. We get stung only once, indulging in a lifelong honey pain. No knee-jerk reflexes. Just a dissembling mental jerk-off, occasionally.

Therefore, we're better off staying, *sticking around.* Not leaving *our* land, unless kicked out by a sustainable *ethnical cleansing,* blazing a trail of blood and tears. Because the story needed to be sanitized to avoid one's pangs of conscience.

It all comes down to having a kennel from which one can bark one's fill. But also knowing one is to *leave the building* some day, losing the pride of places wherefrom one dominates or not.

Ave Caesar, morituri te salutant...

BEAT THE SYSTEM OR—NOT

I'm afraid, right off the bat, my offer won't sound attractive.

But I won't sugarcoat it into a sweet verbal portrait that sells.

Here I am, *a man*—is that where *Amen* comes from?—closing in under arrow flights of years, wielding my 48 blunt and harmless sabers, thinking *I have nothing to show for.*

Totally not of this world, as in not of *this system,* I witness a slow black train of change coming, and I wonder why, for Christ's sakes, *if nothing else mattered,* people don't get a grip and learn from their own mistakes?

Most of them do it only when their own strength gives up on them, I thought.

And then I stumble upon *Illuminati: The Cult that Hijacked the World.*

I'm not going to even go there.

Everyone knows it, conveniently calling it *a conspiracy theory.*

I'll stick with that too.

But just in case they really existed, I want to say this:

What in the world could one do to change it?

Revolution?

Can I please refresh your cluttered mind:

How many of those we had already?

French, Russian, Yugoslavian...

I'm not going back to *that* either.

Let's put it this way:

How many do we need?

Or, *do we need any?*

We're so brainwashed by *Sex and the City* and *What Women Want* that we don't realize the core question here.

What do we need?

Food, water, clothes, homes, money, cars, gas, computers, apps, toys, ice cream, coffee, beer, electricity, police, army, hospitals, banks, malls, post offices, mail, email, Facebook...

Okay—what do we need Facebook for? Or Twitter?

To socialize from a safe distance, at leisure, befriending or disposing of people with a mouse-click, having the galleries of their lives on display?

Is that right?

Then no wonder *Illuminati* and the likes rule.

Because *you* want it.

If someone walked into your room and, as of this moment, asked you to hand over your phones and computers, you'd feel as if it were the end of *your* world, feeling as if one pulled a rug under your shaky feet.

But what are you going to do if there's a massive black out and *all* the power is gone?

Nothing.

Exactly.

There's nothing you *can* do.

So I understand you. It's okay. You don't know any better.

You do what you're told, and a little extra on the side.

Therefore *no* revolution can help you.

Therefore I don't feel sorry for you anymore.

It is what it is.

We're ruled by *Illuminati?*

Fine.

Somebody's got to rule, be it a King, Prime Minister, or High Inquisitor.

We still haven't reached the level of high consciousness and, although I disagree with him on many issues, here I have got to hand it to Nietzsche when he wrote that...

One would rather go back to the beasts than overcome man.

First of all, God is not *dead,* our hearts are.

Figuratively *and* literally.

But second, the beasts cause much less problems than men. They are nobler in their purpose, and so it's derogatory to consider them lesser beings, because *we* are the monsters at need.

Third, *to overcome man* is out of question because it's disproportional, since we, *as we are,* are not even aware of any benefit that could possibly result from it.

As long as we think in *go-get* terms of material gain, our spiritual options are cut off.

There is nothing *hip* and *hop* about it unless you started spiritual level hopping. But for that one needs an *unbearable lightness.* And you have not solved the question of your own body weighing you down yet.

You are to first get a job and a house and friends and a relationship and a book club and a dog before you lose it all.

I'm not even mentioning beer-chugging and chest-painting. Because not everybody in this world does it. The same as not many people sport corn hats.

Not many are had over a barrel of oil, although they only like to think so.

Those grew up in edgy suburbs ruled by nervous cities with no room for errors. They are immobilized by wrong moves, aiming high, lying low, finding pleasure in being praised, honoring instant gratification, scared to commit, imprisoned by high bills that they pay with free checking, fearing their own shadows, needing to feel that nothing could possibly go wrong...

That barrel of oil they want to have nothing to do with indirectly became the main reason why their spiritual poverty is the byproduct of material prosperity.

Until one comes up with a different source of energy.

But the principle remains the same.

Energy is *everywhere*.

It's how you use it that matters.

Thus beating systems doesn't help, turning it into time and energy waste, which again is *relevant*, since energy will just change its shape.

Since you are amazed by shape shifting, *it's what energy does*. And you too, every day. You put some energy in, and some goes out, until one day you exhale it all.

The same way you make love, the more you do it, the less you have energy *and* interest for anything else.

It's what you engage yourself in that becomes *engaging*.

That's what they mean when they say *moderation is the key*. So that you could do *other* things.

Sex is not everything. Food is not everything. Diamonds are not everything. Clothes, cars, cigarettes, drugs are not everything…

But they can become *a little bit of* something until they amount to *nothing*.

That's your *per aspera ad astra* in order to achieve *higher consciousness,* which is *nothing.*

A big O, round and empty. Call it *Zen* or *Nirvana,* or *Mother of God,* or just plain *Nothing.*

Let's repeat one more time, in case your mind is drifting:

A little bit of *Everything* equals *Nothing.*

To *be* in that equation, you are to equally partake in both sides.

As Lao-Tse had nicely put it:

Therefore just as we take advantage of what is, we should recognize the usefulness of what is not.

It's like climbing Mount Everest.

You do the whole nine yards, eventually reaching the top, breathless or legless or mindless, or all of it together.

You enjoy your little victory for a while, realizing how infinitesimal you are standing there on top of the world. Exalted you hold on to a flag that you are to stick in the ground or up your ass, wherever your patriotic sentiments are, and then eventually you start descending.

Every little bit of the entire endeavor soon amounts to nothing.

Of course, you can be proud of yourself for years, your wife can love you more and fuck you better, or maybe leave you, or what have you.

You can get up and do it again, perhaps, as it becomes your *Why.*

You can train people to do the same, or something else. But the time goes by and you are to face your final departure.

This world was fun, you used up your points, your free coffees, did all the things on your bucket list, read your most favorite books a few times each, loved your wife and kids and pets dearly, or not.

According to Hemingway, *what is moral is what you feel good after, and what is immoral is what you feel bad after,* and now...it's time to go.

I know everybody knows, but many avoid thinking about it.

They just want to pretend it's something that happens to others, *elsewhere.*

They become frantic about *living to the fullest,* as if life was a huge sale and they make sure they don't miss any of it.

They want to die a painless death in their sleep and then end up in a dream of their choice.

Sure, that could work.

But for that you need *peace* and *joy.*

Which doesn't mean a *pizza* and a *toy* for the members of *Low Consciousness Society.*

Lifestyle developers will tell you to hit the gym, or build your self-esteem by working an extra hour. In other words: keep pumping as if your heart were an *ARCO* filling station attendant.

There's nothing wrong with the gym or working over-time, most of the world does it this very moment.

You can do yoga as well.

I bike.

It's when my thoughts interact inside my head like bees and butterflies.

I can almost see them effortless and noiseless.

Every time for a moment I regret not carrying a Dictaphone, but then I think it's better just to let them *bee.* Those that are really meant to stick around, they will.

For example, lately I've been thinking how unexpectedly my life unfolded, as many things did not happen. But the outcome is nonetheless rewarding.

Maybe I'm not famous, but I live like an artist. Or a philosopher. Even a hermit of some sort.

I mainly keep myself company. After I lived on three different continents and realized that people suffer the same fate.

Nobody gets out of here alive.

I socialize seldom and most of my outings consist of biking and shopping, which are at times combined. I'd rather bike then drive our old, handicapped car, saving it for rainy days.

Gas is dear too. Those days are over when one could fill her up for $20. I bike up and down the *Spring Water Corridor* past one of the *lucky* 500 companies, and every time I feel *luckier* for not having to be inside producing one of their highly demanded products.

They might make good money, but they also spend a fair bit of time doing it. They surely have better cars than mine, all sparkling shiny parked in a designated area.

They didn't make a name for themselves, so they didn't have to give anything up, I'd think passing by. But then again it seemed they gave up hell of a lot of free time at least.

And look who's talking!

I didn't really make a name for myself either, although I tried, giving up a few things here and there. I still wound up with lots of free time on my hands. Time that I mostly use for typing these conceptual little units of language multiplying like viruses.

Penny for you thoughts, I thought to price them out one cent a page.

One hundred pages, $1. Two hundred pages, $2.

Well, the price for my last book is $3.99 for almost three hundred pages, and still nobody is buying it.

When I think of all the sleepless nights putting it all together, and all the sleepless nights when it was all happening for real, then it's—*priceless.*

And it is. Therefore I don't make any money on it.

What I do, I write *this.*

I thought to price it $1 a book, like a good old cheeseburger.

I could call it a *cheese-book.*

Still I don't think anyone would buy it.

I need a more positive attitude?

Maybe. I tried it all, and now that I know a book is a portal to another dimension, I seem to be one foot here and the other already *there.*

Something happened after nothing did.

I started feeling *different.*

Not that I didn't care as in *I don't give a hoot.* I just didn't.

Even if I sold a million copies now, it wouldn't change anything. Because people would still be the same. And they become shallower and more stupid every day. It's as if they were secretly hooked on some brainwashers in their sleep, and the next day they wake up dumber.

But it doesn't happen in their sleep, I figured. It's their daydreaming that's saturated.

Too many carrots dangling on too long sticks, and donkeys are too tired and nervous from pulling the carts around in circles.

People want to *live,* but many are already *half past dead.*

When they finally reach their carrots, it turns out they're genetically modified.

Illuminati?

Well, whoever it is, it's amazing how they keep selling the same old tricks.

They don't need new ones for old dogs, because puppies can't tell the difference. Until they start turning them, or turn into them.

If going to the gym and working overtime can make you oblivious to it, then so be it.

Whatever makes you happy…

But if thinking about death you feel fear instead of peace and joy, then it's a sure sign that your life is not lived the way it's meant to be.

ALL FOR ONE, ONE FOR ALL

This morning I went to a job fair.

I have nearly typed job *fart,* but it wasn't really.

They were friendly and productive, making sure the music played the way it was orchestrated.

There was no music, indeed, but the orchestration was solid. Queue up and discover, step by step, what's in it for you. Anticipation is a must. Once you show it, you're easily directed to a variety of desks offering jobs from *Aflac Insurance* to *UPS Services,* even *Alaska Fisheries...*

On my way there, driving hectically, I was running late.

It said from 9.30 to 1.30. It didn't say *any time between.*

It just said *if you don't show up, you risk losing your unemployment benefits.*

Since I'm still receiving it—*ask and you shall,* but not forever—I stepped on it, only to find myself in a long line between a guy smoking in front of me, and a huge belly pushing me from behind.

I turned to face him and saw one of his hands resting right where his gut started to bow out, as with the other he reached around, grasping the lower bow right below his navel. I imagined him pouring it onto a table and knocking over glasses and stuff.

I still cherished a thought originated while I drove by the 39th

Street Church:

No wonder we're advised to believe and love God, since He's the only one we have left when everybody's gone. Even though we can't see Him, because we learned believing in His omnipresence and loving it even more so.

Better than this bulging gut *propping me up on my leaning side.*

Once *inside,* we were treated with respect, as they needed some additional force for coming holiday season. Instead of *Santa's helper,* you can be a driver's helper, on call. Or deliver ducks!

They had a batch full of bananas begging us to take them home, because they didn't want to bring it all the way back.

There was the *Portland Art Institute* desk too. One could continue his education and become a culinary expert, graphic designer, filmmaker, or a photo guru.

On my way back I drove down the 39th and there, on the corner of Powell, she stood with a cardboard sign, *needing $ to go back home.* Definitely a young panhandler, but it reminded me of that one time I drove by a lady *with a red-letter sign: a hard-working mom of four,* when I stopped and *gathered some change, opened window and waved.*

Afterwards I wrote a song about it, and there I was again, like a déjà-vu. Maybe it *ran in the family.* Maybe ten years down the track it was one of *her* daughters standing at the same corner and needing to get back home…

I gathered some coins, mostly pennies beneath the dashboard. She was grateful, smiling.

Later I kicked myself discovering I had some more change in my pocket. I also realized that if everybody gave her thirty-five cents—*if everybody gave her just a penny each!*—she'd be rich!

It's all we should to do:

All for one, one for all…

But which *one?*

They can't decide between gods, let alone people…

HER PICTURE

Whenever I feel I was hard done by at *having to extend my shift,* enduring the same old downfalls that went around the clock, I'd always remember my father and how he'd been through twice as much at least. He fought three cancers, he was trapped in a war...

I hadn't experienced any of that. My pain comes from a dysfunctional childhood, and I can hear many of you cheering:

Welcome to the club!

Well, then, let's put it this way:

My pain comes from sheer beauty, and then, like in a song, *beauty comes from pain.* Like different kinds of love, there are different kinds of beauty. And we already know that *beauty comes from inside.*

My pain comes from the beauty of a woman's face.

It might come from *inside,* but its magic is attributed to the outside proportions as well.

We heard so many times that ugliness doesn't exist—it's just another form of beauty.

Sure, if it makes you feel better. But ugliness *does* exist. Or call it whatever you want.

I don't know what *God* thought when he created people and their faces. I can understand what he thought when he created *feces,* but faces, they are our *ID's.*

If you show up with your ears flapping around like Dumbo's, and your nose is thick-billed like a crow's, and your eyes are too close too each other... *Shall I keep going?*

I agree that a beautiful smile can mix it all in an irresistible compound. But that person is to keep on smiling for life, or he'd be *redneckognizied,* whatever that means. We can pretty much guess.

I'm not here to discuss it. I'm just saying that *I'm weak in the presence of beauty.* Period.

And I'm talking about faces, not *feces.*

Why God had created Rita, Ava, Marilyn, and what mold he was using, if any, it's entirely up to *Him.* One definitely can't argue *that.*

But I can't help wondering—it is mainly because I got infected by it, and ever since my life has been in the doldrums—why are there those striking, breathtaking faces that one look at them makes you feel as if you were just a bus boy?

Are they the masterpieces one came up with after years of trying to put them together?

Or has it all gone out of hand, and it happened by a pure chance?

Maybe it's some sort of a mass produced jackpot? The same way casinos are full of handicapped looking creatures, as if someone had cheated on them at birth, and their only consolation now is money that can buy pretty much anything. Because *they know* that full bellies comes first!

Nevertheless, the minute Rita or Ava walked in, all the machines would stop, and one could only hear broken heartbeats skipping through a wishful thinking silence.

Let's narrow it down...

Don't you worry—I'm not one of those secretly in unrequited

love with Rita, Ava, or Marilyn.

One good reason is *they are dead,* and the other one is *I'm in love with their clone.*

It's even better! I got all three in one! I'm looking at it now…

Her picture is on the table, and every time I finish a sentence, or stop to take a breath, she keeps looking at me, the same way, my charming lady.

I *did* find her half way across the world, reaching even Down Under…

As far as the east is from the west.

I didn't shoot that photograph.

I wasn't there when she smiled so gracefully at *God knows whom.*

I took many other photos of her, and her and I together. But I wanted this one, and asked her for it, and she gave it to me, like she gave me her love, and then she gave it to someone else for a while, and it's where the other part of the pain comes…

I wrote about it elsewhere.

All I have now is that photo and that sheer beauty looking at me. Sometimes I debate whether I should shred it into pieces, but it's all I got left from her, and I'm hanging onto it, as if I was at the end of a rope…

Because everything else in comparison with it, *absolutely everything,* looks like a watered down cocktail…

Even my *Why.*

It helped me find her, but it also helped me lose her.

And the biggest irony, or tragicomedy, of it all is that *she believed she was ugly.*

As a very little girl, she was told so by a naughty church organist and warned to keep it secret.

Use your imagination… It wouldn't cross even Temujin's mind.

When I'd tell her how beautiful her face was, confused she stopped smiling.

You say nothing about my body…

That was my double-blade sword cutting me in two every which way I went on about it.

I was first to conquer the flashback demons that reappeared from an ugly past like some sort of shape-shifters only visible to her.

Therefore I asked for *this* photo, still in front of me, where she just smiles away home free, more beautiful than Rita, Ava, and Marilyn altogether.

I don't want to talk here about love gone right or wrong, I want to talk about *physics*.

I want to talk about the magnetic field of that face that radiates warmth like the sun, pulling me in like a black hole. Its gravity and unbearable lightness, I'm hypnotized by it. Everything else seems bleak and irrelevant, although the more so burdensome in its triviality that is *in my face*.

Even when I was around her, in silence I'd admire it, at the same time in awe realizing how much she was unaware of it.

She just *was*.

Her face was just another part of her carried around mainly serving her to *face* the music she often didn't like. And, boy, was it done with a class…

That face could appear anywhere, anytime, enflame a desire for revolution, cause an uprising, or stop an entire war, depending on the mood of a designated crowd.

She could appear next to *His Holiness the Dalai Lama* himself and *fit in* like his additional chakra.

Maybe only *Temujin* could resist it…

Another irony of it—she's enclosed within four walls, scared to leave the premises.

One of her exes might spot her and come running like a mad dog.

Most of them were *psychos,* as she called them, *after* they turned into maniacs of some sort. *Before* it, they were the nicest *decent* guys gradually transforming into *con artists...*

I was not the one, in terms of raping and beating her up, crazy on drugs and alcohol. But there were times I was about to jump out of my skin.

No matter how ironic it sounds, I can relate to those idiots. Not that I'd ever do what they had done. But the way she *faced the music* was definitely frustrating at times.

It's another book's subject. I had written a couple of thousands pages on it.

There you go. No magic blue light to cure it.

You just *become* blue hopelessly shadowboxing the invisible curtains of a show that must go on.

The church organist has already composed an *Unfinished Symphony* of his own and imported it in her *DNA,* molesting her *blueprint of life.*

There's this framed smile now to keep me going sane and insane at the same time petrified in the middle of the scales of belated justice.

If we *just* talked relationships, they are *simply* complex.

It depends on how much a man is a *man,* and the same goes for her, because, I assume you already know, each of us have both a masculine and a feminine side.

The first step is realizing who *wears the pants* within ourselves, the same way we're diagnosed with diabetes, or being told that we won the lottery.

It's either or. They both work either complementing one another, like *cross-dressers,* or hating each other's guts, until they're pretty much gone. Guts. Gradually. Not the same way as in being *gutted.*

It's a slow death resembling those in gulags when fellow prisoners force one of their kind to drink liquid silver, or mercury (as opposed to a slow lifelong release from amalgam fillings), and he dies a painful death a few years later, whether they thought he were a rat, or they just didn't like him.

After realizing you consist of two sides, masculine and feminine, it's up to your goodwill—if you have one—to embrace them both, or shun one for the rest of your life.

It is inevitably going to *show,* and you are to suffer the consequences, or jump for joy, or both, reaping what you sow and what had already been sown within you.

Be aware, *always,* if, say, your feminine side is stronger. It will naturally attract its opposite, unless you are a male *lesbian,* which, similar to a *man-whore,* seems totally opposite to a *dyke.*

On the surface, they don't attract each other, as they stem from the same quandary. What's been grafted in, a wild olive or else, and how much has one become a partaker, depending on how rich the root was...

Too much *conditional* love in their childhood?

Too much *unconditional* love is not good either.

They have them both encircled within *Insecurity.*

One is either not prepared to face the mean world out there, or one seems over-confident.

Both extremes attract insecurity, and they end up surrounded by it, which gives them a false perception of being loved for who they really are, unless they know it, but then it's *sick.*

It's like *cashing in* on it. Which is like cashing in on Christmas.

As you can see, it all starts *simply.*

It becomes more and more complex as it unfolds, depending on our masculine-feminine balance. The Chinese have found it out a long time ago within their *Yin* and *Yung* circle.

It all goes back to a small town *Childhood,* but to our genes *and* jeans too.

The type of jeans you wear shows the type of genes you carry inside.

They both determine your *Why*.

But first you are to *know thyself,* and then accept it unconditionally, which some confuse with *loving and not liking it.*

It depends how *dikey* is the woman in you, and how much of a *man-whore* is you masculine side.

Once you're *peacefully* aware, *it* radiates breaking through the darkest traumas the same way the sun breaks through the clouds.

When it happens in Alaska, or Scandinavia, it doesn't go down at all for a while, becoming the *midnight sun.*

BUSINESS & PLEASURE

It's all about controlling masses, through religion, food, medication, entertainment, and yes, even music.

My ex-boss Patrick was terrified by the amount of power rock bands had over their fans.

He thought they had them wrapped around their fingers.

And look how many people follow designated DJ's! I know one that gets paid $5,000 a gig.

Jesus's performances were admission free. But *one* knew better nipping it in the bud.

Your dreams are also being controlled. In Hollywood there is a whole factory of 'em.

First they relentlessly advertise the *information,* crawling it in under your skin, and then they *comply* with your throbbing desires and wishful thinking that you are encouraged to parrot back.

As a result, people wage mimic wars *and* the real ones too.

Yesterday I read in *Forbes* that one of the 70 most powerful people today is the *CEO* of the Facebook, because he managed what *CIA* dreams about: to *know the most intimate info about 800 million people.* No need to mention their number growing *daily* like a beanstalk out of hand.

The average U.S. user spent a whopping seven hours and 46 minutes on Facebook in August.

This week Facebook had to warn potential investors in its IPO that the more people who access it from mobile instead of the web, the worse its business is doing.

The next news I stumbled upon was:

Mark Zuckerberg Awarded CIA Surveillance Medal

Whether it's a hoax or a conspiracy theory, let's go back to our old adage:

Don't mix business with pleasure.

Discipline is obviously a branch best attached to the military tree trunk.

Here it is implemented as a warning leeway on the issue, meaning you can do it if you know how to…

Mixing business with pleasure can be a tricky task.

It requires delicate balance and tactful strategy.

In order to successfully mix business with pleasure, you must know the boundaries between what is feasible and what is just not possible.

(Doesn't it apply to everything one does?)

No matter where you are, the opportunity for business can arise.

Whatever you do, never try to be something or someone that you're not.

There is no need to exaggerate anything or showboat.

Do not take people's words at face value.

During times of social interaction, people will say things they do not really mean and agree to items that are of no real purpose to them.

Come Monday they will tell you they have no recollection of having said anything.

Many people are successful in business simply because they know how to make deals and interact professionally outside of working hours.

They have learned to be serious when necessary and to play hard whenever the time comes. No matter what business you are in, you cannot afford to be a recluse.

It is important to keep up appearances.

The one about *people saying things they don't really mean* is the best example of the way things are nowadays.

To point out a metabolic difference, here is how Temujin assured his comrades:

As a merchant trusts in his stuffs for profit, the Mongol puts his only hope of fortune in his bravery.

But lets bygones be bygones.

I wanted to talk about *spoji ugodno s korisnim.*

Literally: *mix pleasure with usefulness,* or *efficacy.*

It's what I grew up on, hearing it around almost every corner.

Back home, it's most of the people's motto (Italian for *pledge)* encapsulating their choices. It's how they start they day, how they spend it, and end it. The general meaning of it was:

Not wasting time, enjoying yourself while accomplishing something purposeful.

In Zagreb, there's even a bike route called that way, as if it were connecting the two.

But how does it really work?

Do *you* ever feel pleasure making yourself useful? Or is it the other way around, when *others* are useful?

Of course, it could be mutual, and then everybody's pleased, as long as no one turns into a useful idiot, or a *useful innocent,* as B.R., in his article (1946) *Yugoslavia's Tragic Lesson to the World,* called true democrats who consented to collaborate with communists for *democracy.* Originally, in my language, he called them *Korisne Budale,* which translates as *Useful Fools.*

Still better than *Useful Jews* or *Pocket Jews,* in the Soviet Union, corrupted by high position in the state.

Or *Protected Jews* in Prussia, 1744, limited to a small number of the most wealthy families whose first-born sons inherited that privilege. Other children were considered useless by the authorities and had an alternative to *either abstain from marriage or leave.*

How about being a *useful man*, a male servant ranking below a *footman* but above a *hall boy?*

Unlike the footman, the useful man never enters the dining room or waits personally on the master of the house...

Yet, they all depend on the useful field of view: the visual area in human vision over which information is extracted at a brief glance without eye or head movements that decrease with age.

Bear in mind both feminine and masculine side.

As one poet said:

Men fall in love watching women, while women fall in love listening to men.

Therefore those information quickly extracted at a brief glance are often accompanied by matching words, *verbally portrayed,* or I shall say *advertised.*

And more *pleasant* they look, more *efficient* they are in gaining attention, if not *useful* in general.

Pleasure also has different meanings:

She smiled with pleasure at being praised.

Or...

The landlord could terminate the agreement at his pleasure.

Also...

They take a perverse pleasure in causing trouble.

Like...

I'll take pleasure in guttin' you, boy!

Or...

I take pleasure in infirmities.

But Anaïs Nin tops them all of with:

I take pleasure in my transformations.

I look quiet and consistent, but few know how many women there are in me.

How many men can say that?

Unless they have already tapped into their multiple feminine sides...

VIVRE DANS LA DIGNITÉ

If dignity still existed in people's vocabulary, their standard for living should consist of certain expectations like:

a) the love of their life wouldn't end up with someone else

b) their country wouldn't fall apart

c) their kinsmen wouldn't call the police on them

Once those three conditions proved changeable, a whole new perspective opened, as if cutting a hole through a cinder block wall to install a window to a subconscious mind.

Of a sudden, one could see what was throttled and refused to be lived out.

All along it was buried like a legend, as if it were a stifled resurrection born from ashes. One faced the manifestation of it in word many times, and now in awe he also saw it in deed.

Once one experienced an event, or an emotion, first hand, from then on he was *familiar* with it, as if it became the part of him, or he became the part of it. A realization would set in that a life in itself is but a set of experiences unfolding like a train of materialized thoughts.

Bit by bit, surrounded by new perspectives, you gradually have cut a train of inspection holes in your stud walls to see where pipes and wires are located *behind it*. Fitting all the wanted and unwanted windows, you realize that walls around you have slowly dissipated.

It hits you that even *dignity* was one of them. A preconceived idea or prejudice based upon the rules one built as one went making them unbending principles. The state of being worthy of honor and respect is starkly juxtaposed with *ignominy*. Public shame or disgrace.

Both were generated within an aggregate of people living together in a more or less ordered community, reflecting the basis of their moral judgment. They gradually became accustomed to arranging and disposing of it in relation to particular patterns and methods.

As the standards of behavior stem from it, hence the corruption of public morals, because one seldom prides himself on seeing the beauty in what one has, spending most of his time on a slippery scale between *dignity* and *ignominy* ever evaluating his beliefs concerning what is and what is not *acceptable*.

YOU LOVE WHAT YOU HEAR—AND WHAT YOU DON'T

To the literary and scientific guardians of mediocrity in our culture, genius is always a thing of the past; it may be discovered in books, but not in the flesh.

It's Philip Rieff on Lawrence's *Fantasia* I'm reading, as the plane is desperately trying to break through the mashed clouds.

It was late coming from Newark, thank God, so I could get some sleep.

I woke up not knowing my whereabouts. Outside only a strip of green grass divided shiny wet concrete from the sky, as they both matched their juicy shades of gray.

Just before that we passed the security checkpoint, where the young Asian officer spilled a container of pumpkin seed rummaging through my backpack. I cursed in my language, under the breath, but he could still hear me. He apologized wanting to help me pick the seeds with his blue plastic gloves on, which made my voice raising *above my breath*.

I am to put these in my mouth later on!

I couldn't believe something like that wouldn't cross his mind. Would he eat with those gloves on after he went through hundreds of carry-ons?

It was just another drop in a sea of events that kept tossing me around like driftwood.

My mother's sister is in critical condition in Turkey, as we're on our way to Colombia.

God moves in mysterious ways.

Passing the checkpoint, I look around noticing a new breed of people.

It's not your average generation gap anymore. It's another era, and if this is the Age of Aquarius one boasted about, I'd rather go back under the Sky of Pisces.

Even if it is a transition period, although there's *plenty of fish in the sea,* it doesn't seem that many of them will make it through a mechanical evolution without chips *in their shoulders.*

Their eyes already look loveless. Making mistakes, they promptly apologize, as they keep go-getting. The economy growth leaves many behind.

1% of the entire population has reached 70 million. The common sense, as we know it, adamantly reaches its antipode one is just about to encounter. However shallow and insensitive it might come into sight, it's still better than having one of your hands cut off—where smart phones are still a luxury. In the slums of Rio one would cut your finger off rather than waste time waiting for you to take the ring off yourself.

Shallowness and insensitivity have indirectly caused it in the first place.

Lawrence's *Fantasia* appeared in 1921—almost a hundred years ago—however scant notice was the book received *then,* it is still better than *now*—hardly anyone knows about it, let alone cares.

The other day, I did my first interview, filling out a questionnaire emailed to me—no TV or radio or magazine—it felt as if I talked about life on Mars. It certainly would, had one told *me* about how things went in *Chengdu,* capital of *Sichuan* province.

I could relate to it only *on the surface* of a supposed universal etheric field in which a record of all past events is imprinted, where our traces our forever entangled...

INTERVIEW:

How different was America for you when you got here?

I landed in Detroit first and I'm glad I didn't have to stay there. Finally I got off the plane in New Orleans. That one park in the French Quarter reminded me of many similar ones in Paris. I strolled down the Bourbon Street in a mild shock admiring the laced old houses, finding hard to believe I was one of the best dressed people walking. It was the first and the last time I looked sharp and classy in America. Never again. Pretty soon I wound up in the middle of a Mississippi swamp wearing a pair of snake-proof boots.

Does your past in the war reflect in your writing?

I left my hometown before the war had started. I had dreams about it. I'd wake up in cold sweats. Once I was surrounded at the dark end of a street with a gun to my head. It felt so real that even in my dream petrified I couldn't move.

What kind of writer are you?

I am the old school. Put Cendrars, Miller, Dostoevsky, Fante, Bukowski in a blender and push the button. Just don't add that green stuff.

Describe the oddest quirk you have.

I can't think of one. I guess I don't have one.

What do you struggle with the most as a writer?

The same thing I struggled with being a human. Shallowness of others. Until I discovered *Akashic Records.* Now I know there are simply different levels of consciousness mutually inclusive in a universal etheric field.

As you have lived in many places, what languages do you speak?

French, and just a little bit of Italian, German, Turkish…

What would be your ideal vacation?

To be where Love rules.

How many books do you have on your bookshelf?

Never counted. I need a bigger shelf.

What has been the most valuable resource you've found as a writer?

Finding and losing my soul mate. At first, it choked me to death until it truly helped me understand that nothing lasts forever and that nothing really belongs to us. All we own is our intention.

What projects are you working on right now?

LIFE: Knowledge Of No Return

It turned out I went to *the end of the world to bring the knowledge back home,* as my grandma used to say. It was a knowledge of no return, no exchange policy. Once obtained, I was to carry it within wherever I went. In a way, it was like *be careful what you wish to know.*

The truth is a sharp *Damoclean Sword.* 1931 D.H. Lawrence said:

What we want is to destroy our false, inorganic connections, especially those related to money…

The same year, Dali called his own mastering *the usual paralyzing tricks of eye-fooling.*

In reality, the sun is only about eight light-minutes away…

One thing never changes though. A genius is still dead meat.

One doesn't really want to discover it *in flesh,* unless it's in *a flash.* Rare are the geniuses and rare are those that unselfishly acknowledge a superior cleverness in person.

Things are gone separate ways too far. It's hard to find a *golden mean* between Slavoj Žižek and John Grisham. No *golden section* there particularly pleasing to the eye. They forked like a freeway bent in two directions, at some point in time, until they began juxtaposing one another like north and south.

According to Bukowski, *love is a dog from hell,*

It vanishes like an alarm clock dropping into the Grand Canyon.

Maybe it's just another flower, and its seeds require the catalytic action of water to release hotness...

Otherwise, plenty of bratty kids on the plane.

Their parents treat them with casual respect—the same way *they* like to be treated.

The golden rule is applied: *Do not do unto others...*

Great, so what exactly do we expect from others to *do unto us?* And then we treat little children the same way, but they're not grown ups. Period. You can't talk to them as if they were your aunt Shelly and uncle Bob.

Although, in many cases it would be better than talking to them as if soliciting their views with a military politeness and fake smiles.

Let us beware of artificially stimulating his self-consciousness and his so-called imagination. All that we do is to pervert the child into a ghastly state of self-consciousness, making him affectedly try to show off as we wish him to show off. The moment the least little trace of self-consciousness enters in a child, good-bye to everything except falsity.

Much better just pound away at the A B C and simple arithmetic and so on. The modern methods do make children sharp, give them a sort of slick finesse, but it is the beginning of the mischief. It ends in the great "unrest" of a nervous, hysterical proletariat. Begin to teach a child of five to "understand." to understand the sun and moon and daisy and the secrets of procreation, bless your soul. Understanding all the way. And when the child is twenty he'll have a hysterical understanding of his own invented grievance, and there's an end of him. Understanding is the devil.

D. H. Lawrence's *Fantasia* again.

61

Honey, would like to move over a little, please?

It's how from their early years their parents already create and ingrain a considerate arrogance mixed with a faint chance of honesty topped off by idiosyncrasy of any given system they come from or belong to.

The worst and the saddest part, where the blind leads the blind, is that they don't know any better believing they are actually *nice people*.

By whose standards?

Incapable of noticing *that*, it's understandable they're ever ready to outsmart and mock myth behavior from the old world:

You'll get a bellyache if you drink water after eating cherries.

I've heard the same thing happens after eating apples. It doesn't matter whether it's a myth or not. It wouldn't have become a rule if it weren't causing certain issues in the past. Maybe the times have changed, maybe cherries are genetically modified?

Something is wrong with them unless they are organic, coming from a soil never contaminated by a drop of acid rain and raised by an unbitten hand from a myth *don't bite a hand that feeds you.*

How about that, you smart-alecky monsters? How about a tomato juice packed with sodium? Is that a myth behavior or just plain poisoning?

And then let's dip into another engaging thriller since *what engages you becomes engaging.* You use the same term for *agreeing to marry* and *being busy* or *occupied.* There's not an *l* of love in it, and *so it goes…*like with the perfect headphones:

You love what you hear—and what you don't.

I must admit that landing in Houston had its charms.

We called for a cart and sooner than later a stocky black guy with a short neck appeared steering an electric little train. No need to mention we could hardly understand his dialect. He asked us something about *if we knew how to eat seafood?!*

We were so tired, so we just smiled away and let him drive us around passing the gates.

It was not much more different to the other big American airports, but it had *Pappadeaux Seafood Kitchen*. It was my first time, and the special of the day was *Crispy Atlantic salmon*. It melted my heart. That, calamari, an IPA, and then a strawberry cheesecake… Enough to smother one with a fluffy whipped cream on top.

The captain has just apologized for keeping us *hostage*.

We couldn't land in Bogota due to extreme foggy conditions. We landed in Panama City instead, and we're still here on a runway, waiting for a clearance to either take off, or get off the plane.

A beautiful sunny day in P.C., as far as I can see through the little window.

I'm packed in a tight seat, sleepy, my neck hurts. We've been sitting here for a couple of hours waiting. We left Houston around midnight and it's about eight in the morning here.

Never been to Panama City before, and here I am stuck on a runway.

One *Copa* plane has already returned not being able to land in Bogota. Our captain *Morgan* doesn't want to do that. Thus we're waiting for some fog to burn off.

Bingo! They announced that we are to take off shortly.

Here we go! They handed out some insulin-boost cookies and we're taking off!

Underneath us the green Panama hills rolling topped off with whipped cream clouds. I guess I like this view better, as if I had a choice…

We are arriving to Bogota.

Bellow us I can see a thick off-white mass of clouds. We're passing through it as if it were cotton candy. After that comes green, green grass that could be either in Ireland, Switzerland, or New

Zealand.

Of a sudden the wet gray picture of America is erased from memory. The almighty Sun shines a light on everything so gracefully. The only way to fully notice and grasp it is escaping a dreary fall or winter, waking up the next day surrounded by everlasting light.

Now, this is a challenge. This is why I opt for telegraphic writing in present tense...

I am to describe, going through it once more, our tormenting afternoon at the Bogota Airport yesterday.

We desperately waited to get on a plane to Cali, as I ended up utterly worn out, down on my knees, a few times. Because of a few hours of the total computer system shutdown combined with a sheer lunacy of a misguided management that followed...

And now, *today,* we are already in Cartagena.

Where I am seated, many would wish to be present at the moment, or any given moment in time. It would be a sacrilege writing about a crazy airport situation *anywhere,* as I'm immersing myself in a million dollar view. I am about a mile away from G.G. Marquez's house. I guess just *that* would be enough to turn a few heads.

Mine too, except that I stopped doing it after my life has cut a few sharp corners on me. Now I try to take it easy as best as I can. If you survive certain periods and still find yourself in the same boat you got kicked out of and pulled back in like a rubber buoy, you start seeing everything with a new pair of eyes *and* having new perspectives as well. Instead of sinking, you let the water buoy up your weight. You become a floating device.

You become tamed, wise, and broken-in like that tiger from the *Life of Pi.*

I mean, let's not kid ourselves, when and how in the world could I afford the situation I'm in right now?

It's once in a lifetime!

I said it to a gentleman that came out on the same terrace I'm perched upon, sipping on a *Malbec* from a white mug. Being on my knees exhausted at the Bogota Airport is now just a ticket paid forward to enjoy *this*.

Now, I don't want to sound like a brat, and probably there's more to it, but Cartagena looks like a little Miami, *from here*. Of course, I haven't seen the old town yet, so let's wait a bit.

There's also some amazing fish waiting on the table inside, and I wonder:

Why do I even bother sitting here and typing these endless lines, when another situation is going to change it all, slowly pushing it out of the picture as a new *mise-en-scène* eventuates...

Such is life—a perpetual *mise-en-scène*.

Yesterday we were in Bogota and Cali, and the day before in Houston and Portland.

Life is: connecting the dots between places and situations.

For that you need a bag full of money, or friends of family and friends spread like a net that every once in a while needs patching up, for:

Every hole needs a patch.

How about I go inside now and have some of that wonderful smelling fish I don't even know the name of?

LEAVING CARTAGENA

Y'all know that saying:

Better to live one day like a lion than one hundred days like a sheep...

Not that there was anything much lion-like, as some of it was rather lionized, again I'm seated where I was sitting a few days ago, the same jaw-dropping view, and what else to say than:

It was amazing!

We attended an international wedding, France marrying Colombia, with Luxembourg, England, Germany, Portugal, and Romania involved. I should mention Bosnia as well, since we were present, but somehow it doesn't fit the bill, as it never did...

I was proved right later, as they couldn't squeeze us in for two extra wedding dinners.

Otherwise, when we shopped in supermarkets, the real armed police, or military, guarded the place. Not that there were any recent attacks or any danger lured.

Maybe it was because from our balcony one could see a whole naval base on display. With a good camera one could register every corner of it, but to what avail?

There are three little gray battle ships moored underneath a big yellow-red-blue flag dancing in the breeze. But across *La Boca Grande* there is a bunch of container carriers and a couple of big cruise ships too.

A whole flock of pelicans flew between them every once in a while diving into the water seething with life. Looking down from the top of the building, where the pool was located, at first it seemed as if a pod of dolphins darted out.

The relative mildness of climate and the abundance of wildlife has drawn people to this place for thousands of years. After colonizing it, the Spanish Crown had to invest millions for its protection, building the walls and fortresses around it for about two hundred years, continuously attracting French and English pirates licensed by their king. It was a major port for loading gold and silver on the galleons bound for Spain, also authorized to trade African slaves.

We went to visit the famous *Castillo San Felipe*, whose stone blocks were apparently splattered with the blood of slaves and oxen. It all dried out a long time ago. There was nothing but life and notions of it left to sizzle in the sun. Together with local black fishermen and their little shacks. A few of them showed us around, as we stopped on our way to the beautiful isle of Barù.

It was the only entrance to the Bay of Cartagena, formerly called *Boca Grande*. We visited the fort at *Boca Chica*, riddled with tunnels inhabited by bats. Our proud guide old *El Brujo*, sporting a yellow soccer dress, told us there was once a thick chain that ran under the water across the bay entrance, to stop any pirate ships from entering.

I sneaked out to the little fishing village with an ancient statue of Jesus at its entrance.

He was spreading his ever welcoming hands, his nose eroded from the sun, winds and rain.

I took a few shots of the huts and naked black children playing in the turquoise water. It looked like way back when life first began. The only thing one needed to know was how to catch a lot of fish.

El Brujo was like a stick figure. There was not a gram of fat in his old muscles.

There's a lot of phosphor in the fish, he said, *it makes us very fertile...*

His wide smile said it all.

Later, on the isle of Barù, I tasted some of the best fish ever.

I decided never to touch red meat again.

I asked them to take a picture of me by the boat with *Gracias a Dios* inscription.

The water was perfect. Body temperature...

On the island, there were a few little shacks selling fresh coconut juice. There was a hostel too, with rooms up on the stilts.

A few Europeans sat in front of them soaking in the sun. As long as they had money to pay for it, the blacks did everything for them. Fishing, cooking, cleaning... Still a slave-like mentality.

I wondered how it would feel like living there day in and day out...

It was -1 in Madrid vs. + 29 C in Cartagena.

I didn't make it to Marquez's house. After I heard he moved to Mexico, being a devout socialist, I felt a bit embarrassed, coming from a socialist country myself. I was more *embarazada* with emotions and thoughts, smothered by the heat.

It's funny what a couple of cold gray and rainy weeks in the Northwest can do to you. You're ready to give up your ideas and beliefs altogether, if you had any. Around the 45th parallel, and above, they become dump and clammy.

You're almost ready not to give a hoot about the whole damn hullabaloo, once you feel this slightly too humid touch of a gentle heat. As if it were one of the black mamas massaging you on the beach.

Si, I have experienced that too. Of course I got talked into it,

Yasmine

smitten and seduced.

After soaping and rubbing my legs, first left and then right, she even offered to take me home the next day, and then started chopping my toenails off. I swear to God I couldn't feel anything. But when she finished, I realized half of them were gone. I had to pay double.

She followed me to where I was staying, with her little plastic bucket and her wide black hips chewing an inflated gum while crossing the street like a big old boat.

Yasmine was her name. She had a couple of kids and the pearliest smile ever. Maybe because her face was as black as purple coal.

I could feel every single grain of send stinging right underneath my freshly trimmed toenails. They looked as if a piranha nibbled on them in a hurry.

I had told her upfront I was not rich, showing her eleven thousand pesos I had to my name, and still she went on. Maybe she would have chopped my head off with those shiny clippers?

I gave her mine after I saw the rusty ones she was going to use on me.

She told me a story about her boyfriend beating her up, and then half of the time she was on the phone.

Dear Lord, those phones are everywhere. The poorest beggars have them. Colombia, Turkey, you name it...

The cream on top was when she painted my nails. I couldn't believe my eyes. First I thought she was putting some stuff, which it was. *Stuff.*

I just didn't, in my wildest dreams, expect that I'd have my nails first bitten and then polished.

It' what sun can do to you, and a little bit of tenderness.

30,000 pesos she wanted! 30,000 red blood cells...

It wasn't even twenty bucks, but it still sounded like a fortune.

It's about how much I spent the night before, when we all went out.

We took a *Chiva* party bus first, driving around, singing and drinking *Aguardiente,* so called *burning water.*

It's an equivalent of *Greek Ouzo* or *Turkish Yeni Raki.* One is to normally mix it with water, but we mixed it with cigarettes until the ride was over.

Then we headed to a bar to spend 9,000 pesos on a beer.

I made friends with a guy selling them outside for 3,000 each. I had to come out and smoke a cigarette anyway. I wasn't very excited about all the techno crap and blue laser beams cutting through a pile of sweating bodies inside.

But I did take a lot of photos of the lobby and the old walls. The colors were incredible.

Five Hundred Shades of Terracotta...

It seemed as if the sun was setting right there among them.

You know what happens after mixing spirits, beer, music, and heat...

One ends up in a gay bar.

I am not a huge fan since in the past a few gay couples kissed right in front of me, churning and turning my stomach into knots. But this was amazing...

Two of them wanted to take me home, or wherever, for free. They looked like high-school bisexuals, one of them boyish, and the other definitely a dreamy girl, both having those piercing ravenous sleepy eyes.

I had found myself in a *Mr. Bean* situation.

The most incredible scene was when we all sat around a table, as they tried to convince their pimp to let them take me gratis.

He wasn't much older than them, trying to maintain a scarface attitude, but now he was disarmed and bewildered.

I was like a good old uncle talking them all out of it, tirelessly repeating I had only enough money for another beer and a cab fare home.

I took a photo of them, capturing their childlike honesty forever.

Pretty soon they were called away on an emergency assignment.

I remained sipping on my last beer and looking around. It felt like an off-leash kindergarten.

There was a tall blonde young girl with blood-red big and juicy heart shaped lips just sitting there and waiting for someone to scoop her up.

Was she a fallen angel?

I'll never know.

She got swarmed by a group of drunken dark skinned honchos.

They all spoke the same language.

I staggered out to catch a ride home. The night still felt hot and humid like a huge uterus.

It was impossible to imagine a cold rainy day in Oregon.

The taxi drove me around a fair bit.

One couldn't have it all. A warm night, another cold beer, a ride home, red and juicy heart shaped lips...

The driver ripped me off. I paid 17,000 instead of 7,000.

The next day my toenails got fucked and polished...

It still felt womb-like warm as if inside a whale or a giant squid.

AUTHOR—ON—AUTHOR

These are a few reviews I wrote on some of my favorite books:

Hunger by **Knut Hamsun**

I have read it a few years ago in Sydney, Australia, in an attic myself. I have described it in one of my books, *LUCKY DRAGON & WISE SNAKE,* and this is not a self-promoting, although it may seem so.

I am just appalled to read a review saying *the plot of Hunger isn't substantial enough to stand alone.* In a nutshell it explains the *hunger* of readers nowadays.

It didn't keep me interested enough, they say.

A starving artist obviously became a cliché to avoid. If it were a paranormal romance or an action packed thriller, it would be a best-seller. A hungry vampire wins an Oscar instead. People are not interested in *real* hunger they see across the street. They want a makeshift make-believe fictional world where they can escape their bleak daily grind.

To me, Hamsun's Hunger was a blueprint of my own life masterfully told. True, there are different translations of it, and I can relate to that given the fact that English is not my native language and that sometimes there isn't a genuine equivalent to be rightfully employed.

Just the word *plot* is enough to create a confusion. In my language it means *fence*. In a way it is very true. People do need fences. They need to be rounded up like sheep. It feels like home to them, being in a familiar blockbuster fictional mise-en-scène. For fun, I call it *frictional* instead. Hollywood would never film *Hunger*. No explosions, no guns, no mafia, no adultery...

Just a starving artist strolling all alone hand in hand with his fate.

Well, I don't know many people brave enough to do that...

Apocalypse by **D. H. Lawrence**

It is a must-read: one of the jewels *hidden among the leaves,* burning with a gem-like flame. It is a pure bioluminescence, a firefly of our consciousness.

Papillon by **Henri Charrière**

It is way better than the movie! Just to read about surviving five years in a solitary confinement cell is enough to make your hair stand up. *À l'époque,* I used to live in a cold, cold room, and it made my problems a trifling sum, almost agreeable.

Ask the Dust by **John Fante**

After a while it almost made me believe I was in a palm-fringed Paris *au bord de la mer.*

The end made me cry.

Death and the Dervish by **Meša Selimović**

At school it was compulsory to read it together with Andrić's *Bridge Over The Drina.* We had thirty-three hours on Andrić as opposed to three on Dostoevsky. I was a young blood then and I *stood up* for my beliefs—at home. I read anything but *Death And The Dervish* and Ivo Andrić. Until I *discovered* America.

God, why everything happens there? It's where I read *The Dervish* for the first time—in English. Eventually, visiting a cousin in Canada I stumbled upon an original version, and I stood there like an empty-handed dream-catcher. My own language helped me read between the lines of this masterpiece, and it was the first time I realized how far I had come.

SEXUS: The Rosy Crucifixion I by Henry Miller

First time I read it, I was sixteen. Various traveling salesmen knocked on our door selling Zola, Andrić, Freud, Jung, Dostoevsky, Miller...

My mother kept buying and piling them up on the shelves as if we lived in a portable little warehouse. The books were literally stocked one upon another, and one really had to dig in to read the titles. *Sexus* hit me after Zola's *Germinal,* and before I knew it, I had my hand down my pants. My first reading of *Sexus* was plain jerking off, but then with every new reading of it my hand would go higher and higher until it started scratching my head. I read it about five or six times. Together with *Tropic of Cancer,* eventually it took me to Paris...

Notes of a Dirty Old Man by Bukowski

This is the first book by Bukowski that I read. A friend recommended it to me. Before that I was into Henry Miller. Of a sudden, as if a back door that I didn't know of had opened and *The Most Beautiful Girl In Town* walked in.

Hagakure: The Book of the Samurai by Tsunetomo

This is not just a *manual for the samurai classes.* The wisdom of it is pure and rarely found nowadays. Hardly anywhere else one could come across something like this:

When faced with a crisis, if one puts some spittle on his earlobe and exhales deeply through his nose, he will overcome anything at hand. This is a secret matter. Furthermore, when experiencing a rush of blood to the head, if one puts spittle on the upper part of one's ear, it will soon go away.

Post Office: A Novel by Bukowski

It reminded me of my *delivery days,* arriving at the depot about five to four in the morning, letters and smaller parcels already flying around as if it were a ball game. I was either hangover, or I had a fight with my girlfriend in the wee hours of the morning, or both, and then, after a catnap, I'd immerse myself in a sea of mail. Bukowski made art of it. And then Art made the World.

The Four Agreements by Don Miguel Ruiz

If you liked Castaneda, this is right up your alley!

Toltec means a man or woman of Knowledge. On a pathway of self-growth to self-knowledge. I have recently written about it in my book *Life: Knowledge Of No Return*.

You need to have the life skills to relate to others, as well as relating to yourself in a meaningful way. This implies you are to discover your own purpose in life, connecting with your hearts...

William Faulkner on Ernest Hemingway

"He has never been known to use a word that might send a reader to the dictionary."

Ernest Hemingway on William Faulkner

"Poor Faulkner. Does he really think big emotions come from big words?"

Gore Vidal on Truman Capote

"He's a full-fledged housewife from Kansas with all the prejudices."

Oscar Wilde on Alexander Pope

"There are two ways of disliking poetry; one way is to dislike it, the other is to read Pope."

Vladimir Nabokov on Ernest Hemingway

"As to Hemingway, I read him for the first time in the early 'forties, something about bells, balls and bulls, and loathed it."

FRICTION OR NON FRICTION

I have just written a review on Hamsun's Hunger, and it's fired me up to keep going about my favorite interrobang.

The plot of Hunger isn't substantial enough to stand alone. The main character in Hunger is supposed to keep you glued to the novel. While his growing decay kept me interested, it didn't keep me interested enough.

This is the review that at first made me mad, and then I was grateful for it.

It is a plain and simple explanation why millions of books dust the cyber shelves. It might be a stardust, mind you, but there is plenty of it *out there.*

Wait a minute! It just hit me. I was going to say how people crave more *paranormal* stuff, but then it's because it may already be in their genes or jeans.

Maybe we all come from a paranormal planet far away beyond the scope of normal scientific understanding...

Maybe all the same old *BS* we've been told started to make us sick, as we gain traction on regular basis?

We're surrounded by it. From a friction of breaking to friction between fathers and sons.

We couldn't move around without it, but still we need a little lubrication in case there is too much of it.

Too much rubbing *off* or *in* and *out*.

Then we conveniently just remove the big R out of the word and, as if by magic, we get *fiction*.

It doesn't happen to *us* any longer. It doesn't venture into our backyard.

Although the *rubout* of a rival gang might occur just a few blocks away, or a stubborn stain needs more *rubbing out,* or our neighbors still don't have two nickels to *rub together...*

On the wings of fiction, it's rather a guiltless little trip to *different* worlds.

The same reverse psychology happens with non-fiction.

At need, you put our big old R back in, and you wind up with non-friction.

In space, with no air to contend with, you can coast even at top speed almost forever.

Just include a fantasy based plot with a romantic subplot and there goes your paranormal romance.

It would become a problem indeed, if you don't have enough fuel to stop, or if you have to turn somewhere, or if your engine causes a black-out in your ship.

In that case you come up with a *SF* plot, where the crew has minutes to restore power before running out of air, still missing its target or crashing into another ship, or whatever tickles your fancy...

HAPPINESS IN CALI

It is raining at the moment a few hundred miles away from the equator.

Ecuador as well.

It might be a good definition of happiness. Looking through the pouring tropical rain while nibbling on some tropical fruit I don't even know the name of...

It feels pretty much like a rainy day in Oregon with only one crucial dent in it. Not cold.

Maybe not five years ago, but nowadays it is quite enough to make me happy.

I won't get into the difference between *quiet* and *very* happy though.

I leave that up to Sir Richard Layard and his *Happiness*.

An amazing book.

Like a hungry child, I have learned a few new facts like:

When the brain behind the right-hand side of the forehead is out of action, people can feel elated.

Which means *Good Feelings* reside in the brain's left-hand side.

Before the forehead.

When you fall, try to fall on the right side...

Another fact, according to elementary economics:

Selfish behavior is all right, provided markets are allowed to function: perfect markets will lead us to the greatest happiness that is possible, given our wants and our resources.

The *only* problem in it is that *our wants are not given, in the way that elementary economics assumes.*

One could keep going on and on and call it non-fiction...

The alternative *and* the antonym again is fiction.

Which would you rather have now?

A paranormal love story just a few hundred miles away from the equator *and* Ecuador, a spiced up Latin romance, another cartel falling apart within a cocaine cloud, guerrilla fighters and tortured hostages?

Or a stroll through squalid and overcrowded streets inhabited by poor people?

How about the truth?

Is it stranger than fiction?

Here I am sitting, typing, occasionally glancing through a lukewarm pouring rain. I have gone through my second mug of real Colombian coffee, a boiled egg, and a bowl of tropical fruit all served by a real black maid that is vacuuming at the moment, smiling giddy from the genuine joy unbeknown to me and so deft at just being.

Would that turn a few heads?

Do you think I am not taken aback?

My ex-wife hardly ever brought me a cup of coffee, and most of my laundry I did myself.

No, smarty pants, she is not an ex because of that...

We won't go there, as it's not directed to subject matter.

But *this,* here and now, is the result of a chain reaction. Pure physics.

Like that veil of rain outside. It's a natural circulation. Or an act of God.

Whatever pleases you.

Let me give you an antidote that might oppose and cancel this momentary effect.

I know a few people who, at this very moment, enjoy the safety of their own homes with at least a few thousand bucks in their saving accounts.

They might be a wee bit depressed though, but they patiently wait for their turn. To go on a vacation, to go out, you name it. As soon as the boring winter decides it had enough of their soliciting company that after a while becomes offensive. They make a great miserable couple for a while. And they do it every year.

But look at me, ma', *no hands!*

You can think anything but one. That I am a lucky bastard.

I'm going back to the grind in a month, jobless, still figuring out how to pay the rent.

You wouldn't want a day in my shoes just a couple of years ago either.

Maybe now I'm reaping what I sow. A little paying forward...

But it is not only that.

Reading Layard's *Happiness,* again I encounter the same old adage:

Yet as western societies have got richer, their people have become no happier.

Why?

Because of a self-defeating status race.

Because of individualism being too anxious about what one could get for oneself.

Because of a great need to promote a more secure way of life.

Because one can provide relief for mental illness, but there's still no relief for misery.

Because people respond to one another joys or sorrows through the feelings of imaginative sympathy.

And, because in the US & UK (though not in continental EU) levels of trust are low.

I saved the best for last.

We got nice three *little* groups here.

US, UK and EU.

What's the difference?

I didn't mention *this* continent.

The reason being is that everything stems from the *Holy Trinity* mentioned above.

But let's not lose the thread of our *argument.*

Why the levels of trust in continental EU are not as low as in the UK and the US?

I really wish some of those great, bestselling non-fiction authors would give it a time of day.

But I understand why they don't want to pull *those* chestnuts out of fire.

It would be as audacious as digging into the authenticity of the holy books.

It would cause many worlds' poles shifting.

How about I leave that question open, just for you, the fans of paranormal activities?

I know the answer, but those in charge are too high on their horses to see that mine is of a different color.

They can always pull out their good old ace calling me a *Communist*.

Which I am not. Although one of my great-uncles died fighting for it. Wearing a uniform. Which I won't, if I had any choice in the matter.

According to Sir Layard, *people certainly hate absolute poverty, and they hated Communism*. But unrestrained individualism didn't help either, and *if we really want to be happy, we need some concept of a common good, towards which we all contribute.*

Apparently, Communism is a far cry from it, although *communal* stands for *public,* as in *shared by all members of a community* and *marked by collective ownership and control of goods and property.*

So, what is happiness then, if we skip the power-washed brainwaves that became estranged and keep those that are still genuinely *ours?*

I'm talking about those we can still trust, no matter how low the levels of it are in the UK or the US of A.

Sir Layard thinks it's because their *society is increasingly mobile and anonymous.*

I met quiet a few Americans not having applied for their passports yet, never traveled overseas. As far as their anonymity and mistrust went, half of the time they were mostly concerned about their money reluctant to part with it, being their only tangible security.

Another one of their highly regarded active concerns was putting the fun in dysfunctional. Concurrently, apart from being power-washed, their brainwaves would also shrink fried from too much alcohol, weed, recreational drugs, meds, you name it.

Maybe the only reason *I* can still trust mine is because I come from continental Europe? The south of it, *quand-même...*

Oh, yes, some people there can drink you under the table. But their society, at its very core, is less mobile and less isolated. Less productive, perhaps, when they are *faced with a choice between two divergent amounts.*

The majority, mostly poor, naturally have more fellow-feeling for others. Until their economy is brought to its knees by the *LCM* rule. Their *NRV* cannot be higher than the *ceiling* nor lower than the *floor*, in a playroom where those are too close to each other.

From the standpoint of conservative principle *here,* this sounds complicated...

Maybe *there* human relationship with adversity needs less decoding?

The key to success, both in business and in life, is learning how to become an alchemist and convert any adversity, major or minor, into a genuine advantage.

This is if you want to climb Mt. Everest blind.

Mr Stoltz did a great job, no doubt.

But it's all he did. A great job.

Happiness is not doing one great job after another. It is not about perpetually converting adversity into advantage. It is about accepting it as a part of life without envisioning superior achievements and triumphing over it.

I might climb the Mt. Everest, and I might not. But I still admire it no matter what.

I won't think more of it if I climb it. Maybe I'd feel better about myself doing it, but to what avail? To prove that I can? To who? To the world? To God? To myself?

I was born in the mountains and I enjoy hiking, but I don't do it to prove anything.

I *just do it* without a *Nike* outfit.

TRUTH SETS YOU FREE

Simply because any lie imprisons you.

Your heart must be pure and your intentions clear, if you want to feel a divine presence.

Any form of imprisonment scares it away, because you're not genuinely happy.

I am not saying this as a preacher of any kind.

It comes from my own experience.

I never lied for money or to gain anything material.

But I lied weak in the presence of beauty. As it passed me by unattainable and far-fetched, leaving me gutted. Not only I couldn't touch it, but it also wouldn't notice me, attracted often by its opposite. It would twist the knife in my stomach ending up in ugly hands.

It needed years for me to totally surrender and accept it as an act of God.

It took my true love sleeping with a guy half my size.

What finished me off was the fact she respected him more until, according to her, he punched to death their baby in her stomach...

It was quiet sad she had to carry it dead for a while, until it was scraped out.

Maybe that was her knife twist...

A few months prior to that, I had nearly died, literally ending in an *ER*, my heart racing like a chased antelope, skipping as if jumping over fences. I was prescribed a heart medication and a blood thinner that I never used.

A few months later my father died.

Another ton of bricks... Another truckload.

It was a year when my luck decided to walk in the *Poor Devil's* shoes.

Two years later, I can say I'm *almost* over it. Because every now and then I feel the answering pang in my heart that tells me I had to lose them both, in order to love them the more unchangeably for the loss.

It took a while for pangs of regret to become stabs of joy.

What truly helped me, and it still does, is discovering the truth. Any truth. Anywhere. It elates me like a magic carpet ride inside my heart.

It makes me believe there is a Hereafter.

Before, I imagined darkness instead, as if someone turned off the light and I'd find myself eternally alone surrounded by impenetrable blackness.

It happened every time I frequented between the first and second circle of Hell.

Not that I have sinned much, but I was amongst sinners, and my intentions were lustful at times.

Particularly if any alcohol was involved. Playing music, I'd indirectly incite it.

I am not saying all this as if I have become a saint or something.

But I had reached the point where I could clearly distinguish pangs of regret from divine excitements light as a feather.

I'd cross the river Acheron back and forth, all kind of sins at my fingertips, as I'd refrain from them in the last minute.

I guess I spent a fair bit of time among the *Uncommitted,* although they did neither good or evil. I always did *more* good than evil, and maybe therefore I won a free massage today.

All these thoughts came to me during it.

I couldn't wait for it to stop so I could write it all down.

Unlike in Cartagena, my toenails were left alone.

Maybe because I didn't have any lustful thoughts.

Or because there was next to nothing left to clip off...

A few times, she got very close to my groin, but I was in Heaven thinking about Truth.

I experienced a genuine *unbearable lightness* knowing my intentions were clear as a whistle.

The soft background baroque music, mixing with the traffic outside, had almost put me to sleep. The only thing I had my mind set on was how truth would instantly set you free, if you were not imprisoned by a whitest little lie.

KNOWLEDGE OF NO RETURN

My mother's sister has died. After a few weeks of battling throat cancer.

It was pretty unfair, as in the bathroom she slipped and broke her hip. They decided not to go ahead with any treatments because she was too weak and fragile. They kept her on morphine until she'd get better instead. She was out of it most of the time, allowed only short ten-minute visits once a day.

There is a complex history behind it, a big can of worms. Once opened, it would add another few hundred pages about my mother's family's history.

I'll just stick to *Knowledge Of No Return,* getting and giving information with no exchange policy on it. My aunt *traveled* to it via public transportation.

Now that she died, everybody remembers her being fragile with a premature hunched back.

She suffered a lot...

Everybody had gotten used to it. She shunned doctors too.

She lived. She smoked. She fed her cats.

A few months ago, she got a bit sicker than usual. Having the entire family on her case, she agreed just to check herself in only once and then come back home.

The reason being was that she had seen her brother dying stuck with a tube down his throat, and it's all she wanted. Never to die so.

They kept her in the hospital.

It's where she managed to break her hip in the bathroom.

For more then thirty years she climbed the stairs to a third floor, where she lived, never falling. Just one slip in the hospital turned out fatal.

Now, of course, one can call it an accident or a nudge of fate.

She was already sick for years and at least she avoided undergoing a chemotherapy.

Had she never gone to see a doctor, she would have lived and died on her turf. Not knowing she had a cancer, and not being stuck with ten-minute visits once a day only to wake up sedated and ask what time it was...

All along, the entire family was on its toes about what to do.

For one reason or another, nobody could devote their life to hers.

Now, there is a kind of sad relief that...

Nobody could do anything about it and that she is on her way to Heaven because, the most tormented of us all, she surely deserved a spot there, forever a living martyr and a dying saint.

Amen.

LIFE IN 5D

Carretera al Mar, 26th Kilometer, somewhere in the Colombian mountains. Close to where a famous bug photographer lives...

It's where I have finally faced the Quiz 12 from my online TEFL course.

There, much to my surprise, one talks about five dimension of culture:

power distance,

collectivism versus individualism,

femininity versus masculinity,

uncertainty avoidance,

and long term versus short term orientation...

First, imagine a Bosnian teaching English overseas.

Second, I have already taught Bosnian and French at *Berlitz* in Portland, Oregon, and now I'm somewhere between Cali and the Pacific Ocean, having another three weeks left before my online course expires...

Third, I have lived on three different continents so far...

Fourth, if there are five dimensions of culture, why not five dimensions of life, or ten?

Does it really matter?

We have imposed walls around us for our protection, but also to wall our souls in.

We have roofs over our heads to keep precipitation out. Today I was told that a thousand miles further down south, in Lima, Peru, it never rains…

Houses have no roofs, but they don't open their windows because of humidity and moisture that causes mold to grow on their carpets, furniture, clothes...

Their mountains are bare and they cover them with huge tarps to collect water from the clouds, the same way *el bosque de niebla* does it naturally here.

It's a cloud forest, where much of the precipitation is in the form of fog drip, as fog condenses on tree leaves and then drips onto the ground below.

It's how seven Colombian rivers were formed.

It's unimaginable for a European that a river wouldn't have a source springing at the foothills of a mountain. But today he saw a little creek coming from *above*. He was cutting the way through a real jungle, taking photos of huge *Alocasias* that his mother used to grow in small pots back in the day. He never imagined standing *underneath* one of them and taking a picture of a single leaf covering the entire sky…

Isn't that a life in 5D? Ever discovering different *and* unknown dimensions?

No need for *power distance* really.

Maybe in Japan and Germany, where they have to make sure that *Mercedes & Toyota* stay on top of the game. Maybe here too, where they still have servants and maids cooking and cleaning for the descendants of almighty Spanish Corona…

But in the jungle: *No.* A bunch of clouds sits on top of forests, condensing on tree leaves and then dribbling slowly onto the ground.

No need for *individualism* either, unless there is always one person who will volunteer answers, coming up with new ideas and comments. He definitely will not be from any collective cultures, because he'll always stand out with his point of view, while a condensed fog slowly trickles creating rivers of life…

Now, coming to *masculinity,* it's a barrel of worms already opened.

It can't exist without its opposite, as we all damn well know. But from my personal experience, fitting different culture norms, I have witnessed *femininity,* consciously or subconsciously, being ever drawn to the stronger gender, no matter how much one denied it. If they lived in a total denial, they had underlined mental (which automatically includes) social and moral issues.

No need to get into it. There are tons of paper printed out and thousands of trees cut in vain.

According to my little course, *masculinity is high in Japan, in some European countries like Germany, Austria and Switzerland, and moderately high in Anglo countries. In contrast, masculinity is low in Nordic countries and in the Netherlands and moderately low in some Latin and Asian countries like France, Spain and Thailand.*

Here they don't include my little homeland, nor big Russia. But they do say that…

If you ask a Russian 'How are you?' they may take the question too literally and launch into a lengthy account of their latest achievements or family problems. They are unlikely to ask 'How are you?' in return because it is not a traditional greeting in their culture.

In my country they do. It's a part of conversation, a daily life, a general concern.

If they are truly human, over a coffee or a beer, people will talk to one another and genuinely care. Unless the economy is down and they are edgy from hunger and thirst. Then they might even wage a little war and cut a few heads off. Go figure...

I assure you I wouldn't like to find myself in Detroit instead, among the people with nothing in store for them. Boy, what a crazy world that would be...

Sarajevo folk survived under siege without water, electricity, and bread for days.

How?

Together.

Then I stumble upon this...

The UK teacher is from a culture that encourages competition.

The Korean students prefer to collaborate and nurture.

I have to stop here and take a deep breath, because these innocent little sentences are the simple answers for many complex questions.

It also says that...

UK teacher is happy for students to treat him or her informally and to treat the students as equals.

Maybe so, but one doesn't mention their stiff upper lip...

Apart from viewing depression as a self-imposed weakness, especially those raised to keep a stiff upper lip, why Brits have it and are not happy with it?

One of the possibilities:

Is a thin upper lip an effect of fetal alcohol syndrome?

According to PM David Cameron, one thing is certain:

Thinning lips are common problem amongst 40-something successful men, as aging and stress take their toll by reducing collagen production, which is responsible for keeping lips full and youthful.

So, the trick is:

Smile enough to show your teeth, but not so much to thin your lips.

Because you risk to spread your upper lip *too* thin…

Simply start practicing smiling in the mirror with your teeth slightly parted, as if you are really excited about something, a dentist says, you'll show more white teeth, because the lower teeth won't be hiding behind the uppers, and your smile won't look forced…

Forgive my Mediterranean mentality, but is this why I found many western smiles only seeming genuinely excited?

My email is included on the tittle page of this book. Please feel free to enlighten me. I have spent a quarter of a lifetime discovering why the sun never set on the British flag, and it may be a too old and overrated saying, since the king of Spain had already used it:

A solis ortu usque ad occasum.

Or…

From the rising of the sun to its setting.

My favorite is:

Upon whose subjects the sun never sets.

But let's forget about the old empires and just talk about cultures and languages nowadays…

We'll realize that even if the sun does set on its flag, Spanish is second only to Mandarin, being the official language of 24 different countries.

English might be third officially, but on a day-to-day basis it is spoken in about 70 countries, and there is a billion of people learning it, so…

Who said that the sun will ever set on the *English* flag?

The amazing fact that myself is to obtain a TEFL certificate should be enough to realize that *English* rules.

It's an official language on every single ship and airplane navigating the planet right now.

Talking about stiff upper lips…

Let's move on to *uncertainty avoidance.*

If you teach uncertainty avoiders, *they like planned and structured activities and seek rules.*

They may also be intolerant of the views and cultures that are different from theirs.

They prefer traditional ways.

They are higher in Latin countries, in Japan and in German speaking countries.

They are lower in Anglo, Nordic and Chinese culture countries.

Apparently, the UK people are likely to enjoy new challenges and changes…

Ever been to England?

I came there from France for an internship.

The moment we broke through the gray purée of clouds landing, I regretted seeing the old grim patch of land coming at us.

I cherished only a few times spent in London, but even then once I nearly froze to death.

I fell asleep on the train, going back to Welwyn Garden City, which is a very strong name for a few rows of bleak brick buildings surrounding the *Weet-Bix* factory.

It cost me ten pounds one way.

I woke up in Peterborough, about 2 a.m.

It was the last train. I had to kill a few hours within a frozen waiting stand.

As a European citizen in the United Kingdom, I assumed I could ask the station manager for a little warmth of his cozy heated office.

I smiled at him, as I was taught by my English teacher…

Smile and the world will smile back at you!

He looked a pale enough grown mustache man. I thought there was no reason for him not to smile back.

He didn't have a stiff upper lip. His entire face was stiff. His mustache neatly brushed stood out in the cold like two branches of a black tree.

Not only he didn't smile back. He also wouldn't let me in.

I could feel a bit of warmth coming out of his office and touching my fingers, while I hung onto the door knob so cold I thought it burned.

No, sir, you'll have to go back to the waiting room...

He was from India. A very proud clerk indeed. When I told him there was no heating there, he just shrugged his shoulders swiftly adding:

It is not my problem...

I could not believe my ears! So what if I freeze to death?

Well, that's going to be my problem then...

He just shut the door behind him.

I'll never forget that night. There were a few black cabs waiting outside, 80 Pounds Sterling each.

I hadn't seen that much money in a long time.

I don't know how, but I managed to *kill* a few hours without being killed.

Maybe because of those minus twenty winters that shackled Sarajevo, when I played in the snow, my fingers turned blue, dreaming about warmer places...

The Indian station manager didn't let me in, but a Scottish locomotive engineer was eager to. He couldn't though, because the Indian Station Chief said a firm *No* again.

I guess I was too numb and hypothermic to do anything. The Scottish guy smiled friendly back at me waving. A big hot mug of coffee smoked away like a bonfire in his other hand.

There was another guy in that waiting little shack sleeping. I just looked at him in disbelief, thinking:

If he's okay, then I should be too...

Somehow I survived and got on the first morning train.

The only dent in it was, being so frozen through, I fell asleep again, ending up back in London.

When I had finally reached Welwyn Garden City, I had to walk by the Weet-Bix factory.

It released a big gray stinking cloud all over the big gray sky. It looked so depressing that I thanked God I was to leave that place in a few weeks. I didn't understand how could anyone sane live there...

Talking about the five dimensions of culture, the last one is *long term orientation.*

It fits the bill here, right on the spot.

The more long-orientated students are concerned about losing face.

I don't know how things are in China, Korea, and Japan, but in *WGC* I was more worried about losing my faith in life that happened elsewhere.

I was yet to find out where.

I was yet to break away from *Traditional Crown Molding Techniques.* A never ending tug of war between Britain, France, and Spain that stemmed from the values of long-term commitments between the royal families. Bourbons, Habsburgs, and the likes, more readily accepted change and took greater risks only when gold was in equation.

I was to go farther west, and lose more teeth.

Many English and Irish had done it too, not because they *enjoyed new challenges and changes* so much.

It was because of the Potato Famine, a *blight of unusual character.*

Many were transported by derelict ships for *stealing a loaf of bread.*

People in Sarajevo, *those respecting tradition and strong work ethics where long-term rewards were expected as a result of today's hard work,* waited patiently in lines, under a three-year sniper's barrage, when not only *the infected were taken out.*

Doctors Without Borders knew more about it but couldn't do much.

The five-dimensional model of culture was then reduced to bare surviving.

But life, as we didn't know it, went on.

FROM SAN ANTONIO TO *SALSODROMO*

To discover parallel universes, one is to cross the Greenwich Mean Time and the Equator.

A play on words here is inevitable, as Time can be Mean and *mean.*

One goes as far as the east is from the west to embrace it.

On your way back, after your equatorial crossing baptism is reinforced, you are to detour and stick to a latitude, altitude, and attitude between 25N and 25S.

Take me for an example.

Born at the end of a cold winter, when snows turn into a mushy and slurry carbonated slush.

All I remembered and looked forward to were the summer holidays at the Adriatic coast.

When forty years later I found myself walking up and down the narrow lanes of San Antonio in Cali, I witnessed a few striking déjà-vus from my childhood in an old town part of Sarajevo.

I lived there my first couple of years and then, after we moved to Koševsko Brdo, I kept coming back, visiting my grandparents weekly.

Those lanes became the veins leading into my heart, or rather my solar plexus.

Imagine my jaw dropped to the floor when forty years later, in San Antonio, Cali, I found myself in a similar labyrinth...

The only difference was the one I always dreamed off. It never snowed.

But there were other differences too.

From God, you always get the good with the bad.

You just need not to look at the gift horse in the mouth.

Something your grandma always told you, but you were to experience it on your own skin.

Then you get used to the bad too. The same way the poor and homeless do.

I saw a girl in the park literally tiding up a few square feet of a lawn where she was going to lay down and rest. She picked up every little piece of trash, threw it in a can, and prostrated on the ground a sheet that was not necessarily white.

She seemed very peaceful, *at home* so to say.

Maybe because the ground was never cold.

I talked to an ear doctor the other day. My ear was stuffed with wax that he was to pump out with a mean looking syringe.

He was so peaceful and relaxed that I only felt an occasional sharp pressure on my ear drums without an additional external frustration that may have complicated it.

I don't go out much, he said, *I stay home playing tennis with my son...*

We talked about the situations in our countries. His English was broken like a cute little piggy bank, but I was relieved that at least somebody spoke it. Here only the upper middle class seemed to be using it in the same way one would use Latin back home.

He asked me about Bosnia.

Everybody was always curious and puzzled about it.

Amongst other very popular details that most of you already know, I told him that no matter how bad things were, I never saw any body living in the streets there, as opposed to a wide and very vivid amount of poverty here.

I took a photo of a guy literally sleeping squeezed within a makeshift room made of two fruit crates. On a sidewalk that appeared like a bank of the river of cars.

People are happy here, he smiled like a sacred monkey.

He really believed it.

Maybe because he was doing fine, working every other day, playing tennis with his son, having his meals served, his dishes and clothes washed...

I believed him too.

The servility and poverty are a classic inbred here.

They killed Che, Castro died, Chavez looks puffed out...

The peasants are content enough to find a piece of land where they can live and work for free, serving their lords only during weekends, otherwise surrounded with the most bird species on Earth.

Black people also seem okay with cooking and cleaning, scraping left overs and living in shacks.

According to *The Guardian* and *BBC,* Colombia is the second happiest country in the world.

Here is the list:

Vanuatu

Colombia

Costa Rica

Dominica

Panama

Cuba

Honduras

Guatemala

El Salvador

Saint Vincent and the Grenadines

Happiness seems to be concentrated around the Columbo's first landing.

I still feel a bit uncomfortable when a maid asks me what I want for breakfast though. She also seems out of place when I just crack and egg and drink it in one gulp.

My socialist upbringing and my moving around the world mostly on my own taught me to live self-sufficiently and lonely at the same time.

Finding myself in a Spanish speaking country, I felt more awkward then somewhere in Africa, where most of the people would at least understand English or French.

The biggest hit was the *Salsodromo.*

Literally under the belt.

Again I was with the friends of friends.

The same old *it's not what you know, it's who you know,* followed me everywhere I went.

I ended up in a car with bulletproof windows.

The saddest thing about it is that some of them one couldn't open.

I felt like a fish within an unbreakable tank.

Unexpectedly my friends of friends were a Mayor's family this time.

I was in the same car with his son and his wife.

We were escorted by the real policemen on motorbikes milling through the most colorful crowd of people I ever saw.

Only Turkey could compare with it to some extent...

But this was *Salsodromo,* something like a Rio Carnival, except that these were the best salsa dancers in the world.

I had a front row view, and I wished it weren't that close.

I could see firsthand the most beautiful mulatto girls ever dressed like glittering peacocks.

They smiled at me graciously while I was shooting at them with my camera.

Their dancing was like staccato blazes of fire licking invisible spirits. Their sparkly soothing beings within their divine bodies were the most perfect cloning one could wish for.

Something happened to me that afternoon. As if I was allowed to freely watch unattainable royal possessions unable to touch them.

Oh, yes, they smiled at me ever kindly, those latte angels, but it made matters worse.

I have realized what I'd been missing most of my life, and it was a bit of a late discovery.

I was in a place where money talked, and I hardly had any. Moreover, I couldn't even speak the official language. I wasn't that young either, inconveniently ran out of all the wild dreams.

At least my old teeth got fixed, and instead of one on my head, I ended up with fourteen crowns in my mouth. Albeit, prior to the *coronation,* I swallowed two provisional ones, eating *Pizza Romana.*

I could still pass for a millionaire though, had I hailed a cab in the street.

Literally. *El paseo millonario es un caso particular.*

The cab driver is followed by a gang on the motorbikes, as they escort you to a handy ATM, where you are to withdraw all your money and hand it out, if you want to live.

Or this is how *The Canaries* do it...

El modus operandi de 'Los Canarios' se basaba en que una vez la persona se subía al taxi, cambiaban la ruta que indicaba el pasajero y en un determinado lugar preestablecido por los delincuentes, el conductor del taxi detenía el vehículo donde tres sujetos abordaban el carro, y se trasladaban a cajeros bancarios intimidando a sus victimas con armas de fuego.

Another one of their buddies might be also working in the same bank where your account is opened.

A friend of a friend, in Bogota, had just received a big credit the day she stopped a taxi, going home after work. She could only get a specific amount like, say $300 a day. What follows is that she'd be kidnapped for the time being and every day forced to a money-machine until her credit was gone.

No need to mention she'd still have to repay it.

Thus she did something desperate, brave, and crazy at the same time.

She knew, had she entered the wrong numbers thrice, the ATM would withhold her card.

Since they couldn't get anything out of her, they'd beaten the socks off of her.

Her *lucky strike* were that she, for some reason, wasn't killed.

The next day she came to work with her black eyes and all, her money intact.

I wonder if they'd spare me though, finding out I was just an unemployed gringo...

I could still remain in a bulletproof car awestruck by the amazing living pictures of *Salsodromo* and wait to be woken up somewhere along the 45th parallel, where people daydreamed by cozy fireplaces enjoying their favorite works of fiction.

EL CARMEN, COLOMBIA

Life is a multidimensional reality.

Like a novel that lends itself to multidimensional readings.

5D, 10D, 100D...

You name it after as many of them you have been through.

I used to *recognize* Truth and be all excited and upset about it at the same time.

Not because I *discovered* it. Because other people couldn't see it.

I thought it was universal for everybody to touch and feel it, *simultaneously*.

But there are different levels of it, like in a high-rise in front of you.

Every little box, every little file contains an additional data, an additional piece of a jig-saw puzzle that make up that whole.

I was in Colombia once before, and here I am now.

It is still the same place, but I see it with a different pair of eyes.

Then, I couldn't wait to leave. It seemed dirty and poor. There were *better* places to be.

After *veni & vidi*, shedding my dead skin in all of them, eight years later I'm back. It's like entering the same crowded room, seeing *new* parts of it for the very first time.

Okay, I have never been to El Carmen before. But there another familiar picture hits me. A retired Canadian and an Oregonian happily running an organic farm.

It's like you come to a place you have already seen, and you see something new.

Or you wind up where you have never been, and you see something familiar.

It keeps adding layers of new and old dimensions interacting like a cake that exists thanks to each and every one of them.

An unlimited amount of undeletable data keeps getting stored in a universal etheric field that, because of the anti-gravity, expands like a gigantic *Google*.

You're probably more interested in hearing about beautiful El Carmen and organic kale growing there all the way from Oregon.

The owners were lucky enough buying a very cheap piece of land some thirty years ago, stumbling upon a real precious and clean water well included.

Today I saw an endless line of cars full of people coming to refresh themselves with cool water, escaping the tropical heat. As opposed to minus something in Chicago right now.

Eight thousand pesos a person and at least two hundred cars waiting to get parked.

Do the math.

Why would anyone want to be in the US of A, freezing their ass off and working for the man every night and day?

Particularly after the last night, after watching *Ides of March*, where one praised experts specialized in *earning people's respect by making them mistake their fear for love.*

In El Carmen, if there were any skillful controlling and handling, it came from a smart retired Canadian that turned nature into business. He kept it low key, nothing fancy. A pool full of happy locals amongst kale, beans, basil, strawberries, palm trees...

I know... It sounds like *Paradise*.

It was.

One could even hear Van Morrison through the invisible speakers.

THE ROAD TO BUENAVENTURA

Such is life.

When you think it ran out on you, there is more of it unwinding like an endless ball of yarn, just around the corner.

Today we got up at 6 a.m. and hit *La Carretera al Mar,* going west.

On our way to a *Good Fortune.*

Or, shall I translate it as a *Good Venture?*

We were to rise and shine before the long convoys of buses and trucks formed ahead of us.

We also were to come back before dark in case the *FARC* tried to set up a roadblock again, as they did in February last year between tunnels two and three, when fortunately the army was present and they couldn't pull it off.

Descending downhill to meet the *Dagua* river, we emerged out of the morning fog that gradually burned off, as we continued on toward *San Cipriano.*

Not sure if it had to anything with the *Patron Saint* of witches, root doctors, and sorcerers, but along the trail there were a few inscriptions incised in wood, a couple of them mentioning the devil:

CHARCO TROMPA DEL DIABLO

Profundidad media 3 mts.

Te recomendamos no llevar niños.

And…

El diablo esta por aqui…

No lo podemos tocar pero la sombra y la trompa se la vamos a pisar.

One was saying…

ENTRADA AL SENDERO

Temperature media 29 C

El refugio del Amor.

But before we got there, we drove through the evergreen mountains.

It was a weird feeling, as if going through the Drina Canyon of my childhood, when we followed a winding road to Istanbul. Or like driving Highway 199 from Crescent City to Grants Pass, going through the *narrows* without snow.

This felt like a lifelong summer.

People here don't know zero, five, even eight or ten degrees—they have never seen real snow.

Ten degrees Celsius is the equivalent of fifty degrees Fahrenheit.

Fifteen is fifty-nine. And twenty is sixty-eight.

In *tiera caliente,* from sea level to roughly 3,500 feet, the tropical zone, the mean annual temperature is seventy-five to eighty-one.

We had only landed in *tiera fria,* Bogota, the cold country, which is above 6,500 up to 10,000 feet. The mean temperature there varies from fifty-five to one.

We were descending from *tiera templada,* the temperate zone, where the average year-round temperature is about sixty-four.

We were on our way to Buenaventura, one of the rainiest cities in the world with 6000–7000 mm and 264 days of precipitation annually.

86.6% humidity.

All these numbers are to give you an idea about living in a country divided vertically into four regions.

San Cipriano seemed to be the closest to a heaven on earth. Climate wise.

As we had finally reached it, after a couple of hours of chewed up road (they're building a new one), and a few *engorgements de trafic,* we wound up in front of a few shacks and a suspended bridge, where black people *ruled.*

We were getting our tickets for a *Brujetta* ride.

At first, it was hard to believe it, as seeing it left one in awe. Talking about different realities and dimension here on Earth.

Motorbikes attached to little wheeled platforms with benches and a bunch of young muscly blacks running them.

It was an Indiana Jones' makeshift Disneyland.

A narrow gauge railway lead through a real jungle.

I took a front seat facing the railroad coming at me at full speed. Behind me, on the right side, a motorbike revved, depending upon friction of its hind wheel against one rail.

Its front wheel was motionless up on the platform, I could lean on it.

The platform itself had make-do little benches and four miniature wagon-wheels, carrying us all through a few tunnels to *the beach.*

Going about forty-five miles per hour, with all the noise, it makes you feel as if sitting on the nose of a *Santa Fe* locomotive.

If the *train* got off the rails, I imagined us all flying around, but it was worth it.

It felt like a real *free ride* through a pristine world with red and yellow butterflies trying to catch up with us.

We laughed imagining some of our friends back in the States not being able to handle it.

There was no security included. You were to hold onto that little bench you were perched upon and enjoy the ride. You depended on the wits of your young muscly driver looking like a replica of the latest blockbuster gangster wearing big black sunglasses. Only his smile looked innocent, *when he smiled.*

But he was your ride, transporting you from A to B. In between there was nothing but a deep and dense jungle with little pockets of the river appearing like a dream.

And he knew his job well.

When the other little provisional bike-train would come from the opposite direction, one with less people on it was to make way. The passengers were to *get off* and stand aside, watching the muscly driver handling the whole thing by himself.

He was to remove the amazing invention off the tracks one side first and then the other, so that another bike-train could pass.

It didn't seem hard. It was done in a few swift moves.

We were back on track in no time.

At the end of the line a village full of blacks and shacks waited as if we landed somewhere in Africa. They specialized in renting inflated rubber tubes one used as rafts, while big mamas cooked food in big steaming pots with all kinds of fish and crabs swimming in it.

It felt like an Afro-American crossover that didn't make it hidden in a jungle, left to its own devices. The *only* thing they got going for them was the abundance of year-round warmth and natural supplies.

It still had the origins and workings of a world-system that, according to Wallerstein, *is made up of the conflicting forces which hold it together by tension and tear it apart as each group seeks eternally to remold it to its advantage. It has the characteristics of an organism, in that it has a life-span over which its characteristics change in some respects and remain stable in others. One can define its structures as being at different times strong or weak in terms of the internal logic of its functioning.*

We came to *finance* it, paying only enough to support it as is. It was counterbalanced by our self-contained *academic weaseling*.

We were there to experience a *full on* day nursing our idea of paradise and then get back to our lives elsewhere.

But the river was a reason for it all. Ever running through, clean and temperate, it made you want to float in it forever.

After a twenty-minute walk, just as you start sweating and puffing out, there it waits glittering see-through all the way.

Including the people factor.

Their values of partnership, collaboration and results hardly ever underpinned the work they did.

A few dogs, apart from a grumpy squeaking Chihuahua, seemed more noble and dignified patiently sitting in the shade.

Imagining a tipsy and tattooed crowd rafting the Clackamas river, we were grateful happily tolerating a few more pounds and vanity of a *regular* imperfect humanity.

Even the Chihuahua seemed to fit the culture norm becoming a bearable part of the picture, as opposed to a choking drugged arrogance.

One guy, with a thick silver chain, appeared as a potential dealer, but he smiled underneath a stream of water, coming down next to a palm tree and, yes, the big picture was still *positive* and full of life.

How long can one last in Paradise, though?

We swam, we rafted, we ate, we kicked back...

Surrounded by a number of people on a secluded beach, you start needing more space.

We headed back. Where they rent the patched tubes for newcomers, cook more fish, and wash the dishes.

That's their economy. Together with the drizzling rain, a clean river, and the temperature held steady at 29 degrees Celsius.

There was a scene, a teenage boy laughed at first and then one of the big mamas came from the kitchen to tell him off, going through his pockets. She fished an old and crumpled one-thousand-pesos bill. It was worth fifty cents, but she had a go at him as if it were a hundred dollar note.

Stealing was bad enough, but what was he going to do with it anyway?

I couldn't understand the language. Obviously, it was her fifteen minutes of fame, before she was to go back to a pile of dirty dishes waiting.

We took the same makeshift little train back. Our driver was a black version of Ivan Drago.

It was even more incredible sitting upfront and watching the rails coming at us forty miles per hour. With the click-clack noise it seemed as if we were doing a hundred.

We must have looked stupid and childish to those black drivers.

They looked like they were hooked on watching hood films.

There was no way to describe to them there was nothing like their jungle in the world we inhabited.

Definitely no makeshift trains run by motorcycles.

Upon our arrival we took a few photos with them and said goodbye.

We were on our way to Buenaventura.

It still sounded grand, like a million bucks.

The biggest Colombian port and it sure as hell had millions of dollars involved.

But one could hardly see them.

As we drove by its suburban cul-de-sacs, it was overgrown with pouncing poverty.

There was no stripping the copper wire from vacant houses,

because there were no vacant houses, and no spare copper-wire either.

The houses sat on the stilts, as some kind of old fish-farms waiting for a tide to come in.

I wanted to take some photos, but it was too risky to get out of the car.

It was still warm, and the sun went down quickly like a lazy fireball.

The tide was way out as if we were in the vast Bay of Mt. St. Michel.

Or in Cairns.

We could have rolled in it happy as pigs in mud, or we could sit and wait for another round of grilled fish, taking occasional stunning photos.

Maybe Buenaventura wallowed in poverty and drugs, but it definitely had great fish and amazing sunsets.

The next table was occupied by a bald military man courting a local *Paris Hilton*. He seemed pretty relaxed and self-confident, a natural hip-shooter.

A big black gun stood out like a thorn in his side, while his head shone like a cue ball, reflecting a spectacular eventide.

He whispered another firm and funny word in her ear, as she couldn't stop laughing. The smile on his face was winning.

I could imagine those poor privates underneath him, shining patiently his shoes and waiting ready for new orders.

They must had all been silently praying for him to score on his first shot on goal so that he'd come back in a good mood.

No one needed a sergeant rubbed the wrong way.

The Philosopher's Walk

ONE

The old bow-legged Chinese lady still walked backwards across the bridge.

Some things never change, thought Jack, while others come and go like snow.

Again he was smack-bang in the middle of his life, standing out like a Dick. His balls were East and West, or any Tom and Harry he counted on.

Women were usually unaccountable. When on the rug, some acted as if they were on it all month long.

Jack walked the same old path he used to bike on.

Yesterday he wanted to walk around the world.

It was his last resource when everything else failed. He'd just walk to Paris, Texas like Harry Dean. Walk the pain off.

After he saw the film about a few convicts escaping from a Siberian gulag and then walking four thousand miles to India, he thought:

Why stop there?

Keep going! Around the globe!

Until he read the news…

Canadian man walks around the world in 11 years.

Then he stumbled upon David Kunst, *the first verified person to walk around the world between 20 June 1970 and 10 October 1974.*

Everything was already done.

All he got left was the Philosopher's Walk, *Dick* becoming *Kant.*

Heine said that his life story was hard to describe, *for he neither had a life nor a story.*

Unlike me, thought Jack, who had a suitcase full of 'em, but never walked the same street daily, like Kant. People could never set their clocks according to his shadow.

Maybe that's the answer!

It was the only consolation Jack had left. Everything else was in vain. Every effort he made lasted as long as a few deep breaths and heart beats, no matter how bittersweet they were. All the songs, all the books he wrote.

Everything evaporated like morning dew, if it weren't repetitive, night and day, like the Philosopher's Walk. It had to be consistent and durable. Of its own accord. Disciplined. Built like a brick shithouse.

Jack was not into paranormal romance novels, historical thrillers and mysteries. His life was full of true stories nobody wanted. He liked Hemingway only because he said:

The best writers are the biggest liars.

Otherwise he preferred Fante that no one ever mentioned.

Something was wrong with the world. The way *the lightning comes from the east and flashes to the west,* he figured. The Son of Man's second appearance, like the Sun.

It was just not adding up, or was it?

The problem was we expected too much, cluttered by ding-dong junk we had to jack around…

Jack was not happy his name was literally the part of it. He saw a bumper sticker saying:

Jesus is coming. Look busy.

What a bug-fucker came up with that?

Jack didn't get it.

It was the *Holy Dog Shit* people's language that usually end up herpies for the rest of their life.

Jack remembered that one girl warning him about it ahead of time. She was a candy-ass when it came to dealing with her baby. She gave it to a childless couple.

Maybe that was a good thing… She could continue dating three guys a day without ending up in a can house.

He kept walking. He was not Kant but he was no more Dick in the middle either.

He was just Jack. *Jack Jackoff…*

He had five books written under his belt. He was just not good at selling them. Life took a piss out of him.

He kept writing new ones, as if it were a goddamn newspaper.

At least he wasn't on the lookout for a golden shower, or something.

He just wanted to write like good old Henry and Blaise and John.

Even Charles.

What's with this paranormal stuff and mysteries people want to find under beds as if they were ghost turds? It's nothing but a crock of shit! Sometimes it's just a dead mouse!

And as far as the humor goes, cunt hounds laugh only when they hear little cunt farts…

The world has gone mad.

Jack kept walking swarmed by buzzing thoughts.

The sun was shining saber-toothed.

He saw the old Chinese lady walking backwards across the bridge again. It was the only sane reality he could think of.

Everything else was a pile of cars, buildings, and people in them socializing on Facebook or Twitter, their frantic shit-hooks typing away.

They stick to it like turds to a shovel, hitting cyber-fans every once in a while.

They don't talk to *you*, anymore. They don't talk to *God* either. They talk to their Phone. *He* is smart, shining back a bunch of apps at them. They multiply like motley lice in itchy crabwalks.

TWO

There was a reason why Jack walked. A legitimate reason.

Nothing *legitimatastic*. Although he'd seen some amazing stuff, a combination of legit and fantastic.

He was in the second happiest country in the world, according to *The Guardian* (that was no angel, by the way).

There he was granted a new pair of eyes. Literally. From what he'd seen to the actual laser energy applied directly to his corneas for reshaping and vision correction. He could see far away but not up close any longer. He could not read. And now his eyes were dry. He could cry no more tears. He needed the fake ones. Maybe one would finally give him the part of a grieving president…

No sports for a while. Including bikes. Unless they're stationary.

Therefore Jack walked.

He also got new teeth. A mouthful of china.

One of the crowns slipped ending up stuck in his windpipe as if it were one of the *DT* parody sequels.

At first he couldn't believe it, as he jumped back up from a reclining position. The dental chair was still red. A porcelain crown still in his throat.

A split-second he wasn't sure about swallowing or spitting it out.

Everybody looked at him expecting the birth of a baby elephant.

Maybe because prior to that they talked about the *Life of Pi...*

No one remembered Heimlich.

It was the longest split-second in Jack's life, but the timing was right.

He was not going to let himself choke on a stupid crown! It was just not happening...

His throat did it as if it were an extended part of his intrinsic nervous system. Be it a crown or a piece of food, it was coughed out.

Jack couldn't believe his eyes seeing it on the floor. It had a shiny metal lining inside.

And now, no more biting hard stuff like nuts and bolts. No more eating old bicycles and munching on shopping carts. He was home free considering dental amalgam, but no more chewing over. He was to become a fish-eater, although he never cared about meat substitutes on Fridays. He was not a vegan either.

In order to avoid insulin spikes, a doctor told him to always take some protein first.

Jack figured the eggs would be the easiest. He started gulping them raw, but the doctor made fun of him...

You want to be like Rocky, eh?

Jack didn't care, but apparently soft-boiled eggs were better for a more complete protein absorption. It's how one could lose weight too.

It was his morning diet. A glass of water followed by a couple of organic soft-boiled eggs. Then the usual stuff, although Jack continued with almond milk, chia seed, turmeric, black pepper, bananas, bread, butter, and smoked salmon if available.

He was forty-eight and it felt as if the second half of his life went somewhere. Until noon. The future looked bright as long as the sun shed its light upon it.

After noon there was a few more hours left before the darkness would fall.

Gray days without love didn't look promising. One needed a big supply of warmth in his bones to get through the winter. Unless one went down to the tropics to recharge his battery.

Was Colombia the second happiest country in the world because of the climate or the cultural cringe? Were there ingrained feelings of inferiority, as they never really extricated themselves from Spanish apron-strings, or was it because of the plain poverty?

Jack saw many homeless people there sleeping on the ground, even on sidewalks in the middle of rush hour. They washed their clothes and themselves in the nearby river all year round.

Portland had five thousand homeless bodies. When the temperature would hit thirty degrees Fahrenheit, no one washed anything in the river, let alone themselves. Only a few ducks did.

THREE

After seeing a film about Freud and Jung, Jack thought that people nowadays are more connected with the actors playing the actual authors. Their familiar faces make them feel *at home*. It didn't matter if in one movie they impersonated Freud and a down-on-his-luck cowboy in the other. It is kind of *braking in* the personalities that seemed unreachable during their lives.

The more offbeat ideas are the better, Jack read somewhere. Thus if a cowboy played Freud, it makes at least an inhabitant of the Wild West feel at ease. But the world as we hardly knew seemed as if one had to first *Anglicize* and then *Americanize* in order for it to be *redneckognized.*

Jack believed that not many people would be too excited watching a Swiss-Austrian movie about Freud subtitled in English apart from those speaking German. Jewish 82-year-old penniless Freud had good reasons to leave nazified Vienna for London refuge. His sheer luck was that a Gestapo official appointed to fleece him of his assets ended up helping him leave.

Freud liked his freedom in London, but didn't think much of the doctors there...

After following the remark Hugh Kearney made about the puritans in New England: *this world is an idealized version of the gentry-cum-yeoman society,* Jack read that it was not the society they had come from, *but rather an idealized England of yeoman families.*

Further more...

The world puritans hoped to substitute for the one in which they lived used suspicion and mutual surveillance to achieve a tight social regimen and to suppress individual deviance and sin, to exert tight control over the unruly market...

No wonder patients sleep with their shrinks, thought Jack.

He read so much about Jung, never imagining him having two mistresses plus a rich wife that considered him *a good man* that *deserved good things.* She bought him a little boat he could relax sailing on the waters of Lake Zurich accompanied by his mistress. Back home, with his fine wife, they would *serenely take tea together.*

Women like security, thought Jack. Serenity too. Maybe a guy that can keep both in a happy marriage attracts all those unhappy women, particularly if he was a *Herr Doctor.* It makes them feel as if stumbling upon a peacefully lasting coincidence without looking for it. Consciously, that is.

Jack walked down the road to visit his old friend.

It was a new friend old enough to be his father.

We're given the energy and we are to use it responsibly...

It was the first thing he uttered after his angry young wife stormed out.

They had an argument, something about money and *economic responsibilities,* as in who is in charge of being a principal provider.

Cultural differences are fascinating...

His old friend was awed by the recent discovery thanks to his close encounter with collectivism.

He was in his seventies and an avid supporter of authentic individualism that is the core of the American soul.

According to Marion Smith an American actor played a starring role in it...

Enemies of the United States also noticed America's exceptional national character and, in particular, John Wayne. Wayne's rugged individualism challenged the idea of collectivism. Although Soviet leader Joseph Stalin enjoyed watching American westerns, he recognized them as an ideological threat, and the Duke's vocal anti-communism made him a clear target.

According to multiple accounts, Stalin ordered John Wayne's assassination in the 1950s. Wayne reportedly survived two assassination attempts by Soviet agents, in Los Angeles and on a movie set in Mexico. For similar reasons, China's Communist leader Mao Tse Tung also put a price on the actor's head. It turns out that his fictional portrayals of a very real American idea were an important element of U.S. public diplomacy and useful to the success of America's foreign policy... Increasingly, Americans look to government as a source of financial, physical, and emotional well-being. Americans' growing dependency on government (The Morning Bell: The Heritage Foundation shows an alarming trend under the Obama Administration of a level of dependence on our government that has never been seen before. Today, a full 70 percent of the federal government's budget goes to pay for housing, food, income, student aid, or other assistance, with recipients ranging from college students to retirees to welfare beneficiaries.) is both a symptom and a cause of the move away from constitutional government and toward an ever-greater role for government in the daily lives of ordinary citizens... It requires that we tap into the wellspring of America's exceptional national character. We must practice individual responsibility if we are to remain the land of the free. And we must safeguard our sovereign independence abroad if we are to continue our indispensable role in the world.

Jack's friend was also fascinated by the *Apple*.

It was always a mouse-click ahead of us...

After being brainwashed by the TV, people were given all the gadgets and personal assistants to take their mind off of what really goes on in the world. For example, according to John K. Cooley and

The New York Times...

There is evidence that Kuwait was engaged in slant-drilling of Iraqi oil, under the border. As one oil executive put it, slant-drilling is enough to get you shot in Texas or Oklahoma.

Followed by...

Saddam's foolhardy invasion of Kuwait enabled President George Bush and Secretary of State James Baker to assemble and lead a crushingly powerful military coalition to eject Saddam from Kuwait and remove the threat he posed to Western oil resources.

It sounded like a respective intro for the movie *Green Zone*.

Jack and his friend were on their way to a free Apple course. The lesson of the day was how to use *Mail*. Talking about *a level of dependence on our government that has never been seen before*.

Now one depends on *the apple of his eye*, as one always did since reading Shakespeare:

Flower of this purple dye

Hit with Cupid's archery

Sink in apple of his eye

Or Zechariah 2:8...

For thus saith the LORD of hosts; After the glory hath he sent me unto the nations which spoiled you: for he that toucheth you toucheth the apple of his eye.

Or Vishant Panakkal's blog...

The Meaning Behind Apple's Logo

According to the designer Rob Janoff, it is not a reference to the computing term byte.

1 byte = 8 bits

8 (Eight) bits, or binary digit can be used to represent, two states of information;

ONE/ZERO

ON/OFF

TRUE/FALSE

MALE/FEMALE

IGNORANCE/KNOWLEDGE

GOOD/EVIL

The more bytes, more intelligence, the more information you can store or process faster.

So what fruit is the apple referring to?

Is it the Newton's apple that fell on to his head, when he got the idea for how gravity works. Many have speculated that it is the reference to the father of modern computer Alan Turing, who was imprisoned on the charges of homosexuality, in 1952. He was first subjected to chemical castration, treatment with female hormones, and in 1954, he eventually killed himself by taking a bite of a cyanide injected apple. Also Alan's favorite childhood story was Snow-White, where she falls asleep forever on eating an poisoned apple, to be later woken up by a prince.

Or may be a reference to the forbidden fruit in the "Garden of Eden." The bite taken out of it suggest that it is. If this is a reference to the apple "Tree of knowledge of good and evil" in the Garden of Eden, then what does the Apple company referring to, Eve, the Serpent, or may be the knowledge itself (Malum in Latin means both evil and apple). It is apple aligning themselves with the adversary, duality, snake or the Lucifer, the rebel and the liberator of God's monotheistic tyranny.

No matter how sophisticated the modern technic was, it is ever inspired by the *original sin,* thought Jack, while sitting at the free class in one of the Apple stores. It had more employees than customers.

The *Brave New World* kept spreading over the lithosphere with its worst enemy like a mirage on the horizon.

Boredom, and how to evade it.

Distraction with another activity, or assess something in a different way to increase the value and importance of it?

He debated on Michael S. Gazzaniga's quote…

What people find beautiful is not arbitrary or random but has evolved over millions of years of hominid sensory, perceptual, and cognitive development.

And then he stumbled upon, V.S. Ramachandran and S. Blakeslee:

Everything the visual system does is based on (such) educated guesswork.

The problem is that our mind is flooded by perfect images, concluded Jack. It is what is required nowadays for anything to be noticed and, if memory sticks are big enough, to eventually be remembered and not deleted in the long run.

The Apple is *becoming* the apple of our eye!

It had already crossed Jack's mind.

If we switched off all devices *and* our brains, and if we just opened our eyes and *looked*, we'd *see*. The world around us. Every single tree is different, every blade of grass, every falling leaf, yet, at a glance, they're all the same.

It's like going to a supermarket to get some apples. They're all shining wax polished. You get blinded by the glare. You almost overlook those deprived of gloss and luster. If you stop and have a look at them, you get a shock. They're much more expensive. They're organic. They're real. Born in their birth suit. No wax and pesticides trapped underneath it. But can we afford the double price?

Well, thought Jack, if we want our apples without maggot flies and railroad worms, maybe we should recognize their inalienable individual rights, because they like apples too… Unless every man is convinced that an inalienable right to his own life is derived from his nature as a *rational* being.

A little collectivism wouldn't hurt, smiled Jack, in case all those bugs have distant relatives in outer space.

If yes, let's pray they're not bigger than us…

FOUR

A few years ago someone told Jack to accept everything that comes his way without resisting.

It is the only way to follow your destiny, they said, *when your fate waits around the right corner.*

But it could be any corner?

Apparently not, because our way is already charted and there are only specific corners we should turn.

Even when they take us to a death camp, we shouldn't resist, even when they knock on the door to cut our throat?

Those are the nightmares that made Jack leave his hometown, and now, years later, he's found himself on another continent with a lot that happened in between.

Apart from being alive, he couldn't say he was truly happy.

As if he walked around in someone else's shoes.

He wondered, had he stayed, accepting the horror of his bad

dreams, maybe they'd have cut his throat by now and he'd be on his way to the Hereafter... *If there's any.*

So that's the first thing. *Believing.* Accepting everything without resisting, and above all appreciating life, in whichever form it comes our way, and thus appreciating the time of our death, because it is *our* time, our journey—*we* are to travel across the seven skies!

Imagine we boarded a wrong ship, or maybe they all go to the same destination...

Jack often had dreams about the love of his life interacting with other people, while he's around being always a second choice, crucified between her and his family.

In the real life she had already interacted with somebody else, hence his fear maybe. But it might also be the part of accepting it. Even if she left him, maybe that's the higher plan, and if he followed the lead without interrupting it, then he'd end up where he was supposed to, otherwise it's all a universal mess...

Someone told him that if he doesn't make important decisions about anything, someone else will do it for him—life itself. Where to go, what to do, how to behave—or one simply won't be able to express himself within surroundings that don't correspond to the way he is cut out.

Jack was confused...

Does it mean we are to impose ourselves and elbow our way through, or quietly accept the role of appreciative followers, obeying self-proclaimed leaders? Or those chosen by *The People's Vote?*

Courtesy of his family, he got new teeth and a new pair of eyes...

It was their token of appreciation for all he's been through—for them.

Would he rather turn back time and do things differently, or accept it all as his destiny?

He could have taken control over his life, he could have also refused their gift, but it wouldn't bring him back what he's already missed out on...

They needed him around to do things their way. Some people will arrange everything to have one behave according to their plans.

In return he gets new eyes and new teeth. *Bingo!* He also got rid of all the amalgam that's been poisoning him for years. But he was lonely, far away from his love, surrounded by his loved ones...

To be at peace one is to accept and appreciate it all as the part of a plan that requires higher co-pays. Otherwise his soul ends up squashed and his heart walked all over.

People come and go no matter what they do, no mater what they achieved, their time comes eventually.

One fights for his dear life, taking control over it, taking it in his own hands, forced to social climb only to find the Jacob's Ladder leaned against the wrong wall.

Over the years one discovers the same old general truths one came upon centuries ago, like *know thyself.* One falls in love more with the words than their inspiration...

Jack figured we live as if we are never going to die. We live in denial. We act as if life is all about winning Oscars that boost our ego.

We can't take them to our grave. We can't take anything, but we can die in peace knowing that we loved and that we were loved.

Only love makes it all worthwhile. Only in love you don't count how much you give and receive...

It's when Jack checked his email and learned that a fellow English teacher died.

Originally from New Jersey, he threw himself off a seventh floor balcony to catch up with the asphalt jungle of Cali.

After knowing him for thirty years in Colombia, his only friend is not allowed to bury him. Hector has no close family relatives, and his unclaimed leftovers will be picked up by the U.S. Embassy officials.

He'll probably end up outside New York City, in a potter's field, where burials are commonly made without markers of any sort, as the poor, homeless, and unknown are lay to rest by the prisoners from Riker's Island.

FIVE

If Love is not God, *there isn't any,* thought Jack. It should be the only one we worship…

He met Hector just a few weeks earlier, at his birthday party, up in San Pablo, where a few clouds sat on the mountain peaks and wrapping everything in fog.

Mist!

Tipsy Hector wouldn't stop shouting in his annoying Jersey accent.

It's *misty,* not *foggy!*

A few rums ran through his veins and he was genuinely touched by the cake and candles. He joked he could hardly hold back tears.

Deep inside he was crying.

He'd written a suicide letter a few weeks prior to that and everybody thought it was just an attention craving.

At the party he seemed to be the happiest man around. Jack took the last photos of him. In one he waved a big kitchen knife, impersonating a crazy serial killer. Behind him everybody was all smiles.

People were masters of disguise. When they laugh crazy, they cry inside.

A couple of weeks later, Hector was on the news. He made a big mess stopping the local traffic. It took a while to scoop him up.

His friend said someone took a photo of the *splash* and put it in the local paper. His face was intact, smiling...

Jack went for a walk.

It was the only time his thoughts would arrange themselves following some kind of magnetic laws like migrating birds, or bees in a hive.

Mind you, a few flocks of geese flew back and forth, or it might have been the same one confusing north with south. Eventually they'd join the main gaggle by the McLaughlin pond, grazing together with ducks. Until they up and left for Canada, or Mexico again.

People do the same, following their hearts instead, figured Jack.

But when their hearts break or are just plain lonely, they lose their compass—they stop using it.

It's not only *when grandparents eat sour grapes the grandkids teeth turn numb.*

It's when they don't love them their hearts turn numb also.

Jack remembered reading somewhere that one of the main causes for Leukemia in kids and pets is lack of love.

Addictive-compulsive stealing is also filling void in lives that mainly comes from lack of love. Because everything else stems from it, thought Jack. Emotional disturbance, lack of permanence, unhealthy environments, engagement in rule-breaking, over-discipline, scars that cause one to rebel into law-breaking behaviors, impulse control disorder...

No wonder love is misinterpreted, he continued pondering along the Johnson Creek to Sellwood. It's all about war and peace…

Pick your battles, they say ending up in the battle of the sexes. Has equality brought an end to it?

Nope, as long as there is fighting for power…

It brings one back to the same old *love of power, and power of love.*

As long as we think in terms of fighting, war, and battles, there can be no peace and love and understanding, concluded Jack.

As in any battle and war, there must be a winner, or both sides lose.

Hence one sees Love as a surrendering.

But we only surrender when we fight! If we surrender to our feelings, it means we fight them off!

Jack was excited. The rain started drizzling, but he didn't mind. Rain or shine. A pure comprehension outlasted everything.

It simply means that Love is misunderstood. The concept of it.

Exactly! *The concept!* Jack was elated now.

One lives with a conceptual world view, mostly contemplating life!

One expects to *fall in* and *out* of love! One sees it as an active concern!

But love is fucking sacred, *excuse my French!*

It should be praised and worshiped as our only savior!

Without it we are nothing but numbers and automatons, backing our believes with science, while getting tangled up in a bureaucratic mess…

Only a few little birds flew by as Jack figured it all out.

It had been two years since he had any sex at all, and he felt at peace. Lonely at times though. But there was no turf war. No love either, apart from God's all-inclusive one. A package deal for animals, plants and humans. It's how *she* loved too. Jack was only first on her laundry list of complaints.

Her smile was framed in on his table...

The newest research finds that *an evolutionary battle of the sexes keeps the genders in an endless feedback loop of height variations across the generations.*

We are sexually dimorphic, read Jack further, which means there are obvious differences and, *as we share most of our genome, sexes are mainly battling over height.*

Amazingly, studies have found that short women and average-height men are more likely to pass on their genes...

No one mentioned love. It didn't seem to matter. It hardly ever does. Because love is considered a foolish flood of serotonin, a love-struck phase.

It is so sad, thought Jack, that people will always find the right words to humiliate and hurt, when their ego is at stake. But in front of a miracle they stand in awe speechless. There is only one word they can use for it, and they don't know how.

Love *is* God.

SIX

Jack started to believe that all his voyages were but a warmer up for the last big one.

So what with those that never moved outside their local parameters?

What about the American Indians that worship their land?

Well, didn't they cross Beringia thousands years ago during the Ice Age, thanks to the huge drops in sea level?

The current archaeological theory is that they might have come by boat to Monte Verde, Chile. The radiocarbon dating shows that *people have been in Americas for at least 11,500 years.* The genetic research shows that *they share a common ancestor with the native people from south-central Asia.*

How ironic they call white people Caucasian instead, thought Jack.

His father's brother had traced their family tree four hundred years back and found their origins in Caucasus.

Some anthropologists connect *Kennewick Man* with several early populations in Asia and the Pacific due to their shared *Caucasoid features* that include *narrow, elongated sculls.*

Besides the fact that, originating at the same place, the natives came here from the west, and I came here from the east, we still did quiet a bit of traveling! At least they settled down for a while, and I'm still on the move!

Why is that so?

Those were Jack's usual mind benders. Until one day he read…

Paradise, according to Qur'an, is a garden arranged by one's own work and effort.

For a long time he compared it to his father's meticulous gardening in their back yard.

Jack would help him with loading and unloading heavy stuff, or digging in the dirt. But he hated weeding. His father was addicted to it.

It took a few crossing of the Equator, instead of Beringia, for Jack to get enlightened by a simple truth. The *garden* Qur'an refers to does not have to be green, as in planting flowers and vegetables…

It's anything one does. It's the way one lives.

It's going to be all his soul's got to show for when it sets out on the final journey strip naked.

Creating your own garden is like using createspace.com to self-publish a book, thought Jack.

One can DIY it all the way from writing the manuscript to taking a photo and creating his own cover…

One can use already available templates just filling them out properly. *Et voilà!* It's how one creates his own eternal work of art.

Mind you, one is to carefully choose between a paranormal

romance and an action packed thriller that might keep him on his toes forever...

As far as race and racism go, Jack stumbled upon some uncanny facts:

1. *Most people who identify themselves as African American in the U.S. have some European ancestors. Additionally, a large number of people who identify themselves as European American have some Native American or African ancestors.*

2. *In the early 20th century some churches in the U.S. would hang a pinewood slab on the door with a comb hanging from a string. A person could enter only if his or her skin was lighter then the pinewood and if they could run the comb through their hair without it snagging.*

3. *Traditionally the U.S. has followed the concept of hypodescent, or the rule that a child of a mixed race union is classified in the less privileged group.*

4. *Scientists project that in 1,000 years humans will come in many different colors, though people in the city will have a more mixed skin color rather than strikingly dark or light skin.*

SEVEN

Jack's aunt died in Istanbul.

She lived there since he was born.

Unmarried, she followed her parents to Turkey with the remaining *single* half of the family. Almost fifty years ago.

There they bought a piece of land soon after crossing Bosporus, just behind the *Gate to the Orient*.

If they kept going across the country up to where the Noah's Ark was found, they'd find themselves at the foot of the Caucasus Mountains.

For Jack's grandfather just to be in God's country was good enough.

He was a god-fearing man having different views to his communist brothers. Albeit they all followed irrational and dogmatic beliefs in a peachy future promised to the faithful and obedient.

Whether human characteristics were inherited through genetics or caused by different environments, it didn't matter to Jack anymore.

From a *Godless Country* he came to *One Nation Under God,* where *He* had a different office on every corner.

It was like some kind of *Heavenly Real Estate.*

After his aunt died, Jack believed the whole thing was out of whack.

She was the most faithful and obedient of them all. A living martyr and a dying saint. Never married, no children. She took care of a few cats. The only *sin* she got a thrill out of was smoking. Accompanied by ever-present *Rabbit's blood* tea she drank instead of water.

According to a Turkish saying, two pleasures are incomplete without each other. Both are linked and one always follows the other.

Whichever one you choose, the other will string along with.

She had a hunch that she would lose though, her back literally ending in an arch. Because she took the weight of which was already brought into being. On her shoulders she carried the mental pressure of the entire extended family that was shaped by a double-dragon of unscientific beliefs and the daily grind run by heartless capitalists.

Jack took a deep breath after this.

It explained everything in a nutshell, yet it sounded puzzling if one never knew freedom.

It was at least one thing his country and America had in common.

They fought for freedom kicking the turncoats out.

Some remained still hiding under their beds. Nothing could have been done about it. Most games begin and end that way.

The taste of freedom was important, as some never sense it.

Hence Jack preferred to walk, disliking the idea of conventional confining applied by business, house, car, dog and kid owners.

Particularly after he read about confined animal feeding operations:

Newborn bull calves are taken away from their mothers and shipped off to veal producers for a short life of torture. Some bull calves are killed within a few days of their birth, but many are harvested for veal.

These veal calves are typically kept immobilized in tiny crates so that their flesh stays tender, until they are slaughtered at 16 to 20 weeks of age. Their confinement is so extreme that they cannot even turn around or lie down comfortably.

This abuse begins as young as one day old. In order to make their flesh white, the veal calves are fed a low iron, nutritionally deficient liquid diet that makes them ill; they frequently develop anemia, diarrhea, and pneumonia.

Wherever his aunt was, it could not be as horrific, hoped Jack.

Any place was better than a man-made hell here on Earth.

EIGHT

Nobody wants to cry but, when needed, tears are expensive…

It's the first thought that hit Jack with the drops of fake tears he squeezed into his eyes this morning.

It was still dark and he touched his eye lashes with the tip that was supposed to remain sterile and prevent infections.

Too late, thought Jack, as he felt a relief from a 1% Carboxymethyl-shit solution.

The thoughts kept whirling like invisible dwarf-dervishes within a nano-scale, *at which the motion and behavior of individual particles begin to have a significant effect on the behavior of a system…*

Everything is already sung in songs inspired by unsung heroes and those less heroic but still remarkable fates!

It might be the devil

It might be the Lord

But you gonna have to

Serve somebody…

One pretty much goes from one devil to another, seeking what they want to know, as opposed to what they need…

We're already in another song, thought Jack, and it's not even 6 o'clock yet!

You can't always get what you want…

Or another classic from his hometown's bard:

She passed through my songs passionately

Leaving a trace in each and every one of them…

Jack was on his way to a free Apple course on how to effectively use his amazing little personal assistant more and more realizing *it* was using him. Most of his spare time, as most of his time became spare.

A few visionaries put *Apple* together and now *the world is our oyster,* thought Jack.

Last time he saw a bald short fat guy in black combat boots, wearing a Scottish kilt, walk straight through the EMPLOYEES ONLY door. Followed by another post-nuclear individual with half of her hair shaven and the other half dyed green…

Almost as if one was shooting *Braveheart* around the corner.

Jack liked the movie but couldn't help wondering whether that tug-of-war was an ongoing deal…

Is it about Mackintosh ruling the world?

Together with McDonald's, McMenamin's, and other clans…

Jack read that the *Scottish Rite* was globally the largest and most widely practiced *Masonic Rite.* It wouldn't surprise him if all of them had a *MacBook Pro* on their tables…

NINE

An opposing difficulty takes you higher, the same as a plane takes off against the wind...

It was a sermon about how much a man is to submit to daily adversities.

The more you are in accord, bending with the wind, the less you achieve...

They have never been to the Greenough Shire, thought Jack.

There the *leaning* trees are bent like eerie elbows due to the salt-laden winds, literally growing recumbent along the ground.

After seeing that, the *against the wind* idea seems reduced and deflated...

But maybe it's because trees have no choice! They have no wings to fly. Planted they can't move, hence they are forced to bend...

With airplanes and birds is different. The wind adds more velocity to the air over their wings, creating more lift...

With a headwind, the plane climbs over obstacles at the end of the runway at a steeper angle. Because *there is greater airspeed with less acceleration, thus takeoff speed is reached more quickly.*

So we people are somewhere between the birds and trees, concluded Jack. As long as we don't end up smack bang in the middle of a wind rose *too busy climbing the greasy pole…*

The other day he saw the *Iron Lady* and it brought him back to his high school days.

It used to be about trying to do something…now it's trying to be someone…

We are formed by our history, they by their philosophy, not by what has been, but by what can be…

Your thoughts become your words, your words your actions, your actions your habits, your habits your character, your character your destiny…

We become what we think…

You haven't had to fight hard for anything; it's all been given to you, and you feel guilty about it…

The Iron Lady, the grocer's daughter, had said it all, changing the world for better or for worse…

The other day Jack was in the Clackamas ER again. Interpreting for a lady that had her uterus removed. She came in swollen as if she had a spare tire around her waist. She couldn't pee. They had to wait for almost six hours just to be admitted. Jack wondered what the Iron Lady would have done…

Maybe she had an iron bladder, he thought.

In the hallway there was an eye testing chart. Jack wanted to know what his vision was like now. As he approached the chart, it said that for 20/20 one is to be 20 feet away. He measured it, step by step, and then heard the voice:

Excellent! You're way sober than most of those attending the diversion school…

Jack looked at him taken aback, half step in the air, he forgot which one it was, 18 or 19?

It didn't really matter, because the guy kept on talking, as if he was used to having an audience:

It's unbelievable they come to school drunk after they had a DUI!

One would think they learned their lesson...

What happens to them then?

Oh, they take them straight to jail! No more alcohol for me, mister! I was an alcoholic before, but haven't touched it in years! My wife still is though...

How much does she drink?

Four-five glasses of wine a night...

It's not too bad, said Jack. He knew some people drank way more. Even the Iron Lady had a scotch or two before going to bed...

The guy kept going on. One of his eyes was red and open more than the other. Jack told him.

How did you know?

Well, I saw it... Jack was confused. It was pretty obvious.

The guy went on about his glaucoma and not being able to ride his Harley anymore. He took care of his elderly neighbors instead.

Then he started talking about his nephew that just returned from Iraq acting strange...

Maybe he has a PTSD?

Yeah, yeah, he's got those—what do you call them?

Flashbacks?

Yeah, the other day we drove by a fire and of a sudden he started remembering and talking... He said that the worst thing was when they had to go in the huts and kill everybody...

The huts?

Yeah, that's how they called those homes in the desert...

Jack thought that only back home the killing went out of hand.

They did the same thing in Vietnam, when I was there. I could see it from the chopper. The whole village lined up, and they'd shoot them all, women, children... In case they had grenades on them or something...

Or something, thought Jack, but didn't say it.

Germans killed one million and seven hundred thousand people in his country only. But they spared his mother's family.

As they lined them up against the wall, up to their knees in the snow, somebody said something. Jack's mother was still a baby in her mother's hands. In a split second, a few grenades exploded nearby and the soldiers ran over there...

Had they pulled the trigger then, Jack would have neither seen the light of day nor the forest for the trees.

TEN

A month after the surgery, Jack was back on his bike.

Down the 45th Avenue right onto the Johnson Creek Boulevard. Behind him, he heard a shriek…

…up!

He couldn't understand what it was about. It sounded like an accident. As he stopped and turned around, another bike was shooting down the Harney Drive.

Jack didn't realize a guy was yelling at him. A drill sergeant's voice:

You gotta watch when you merge!

It was Jack's first day biking after a couple of months of walking with a new vision. Before he was set back, now he was set up. He could see the light at the end of the tunnel perfectly clear, but he couldn't read anymore. His stigmatism was gone. Now he could see a *drill sergeant* on a red bike ahead of him becoming small like a fly.

Years ago Jack would have certainly reacted. Something like *what's your problem?*

But his new vision changed everything. He was amazed he could see all the way where the trail was ending. Everything looked so tiny in the distance. Even the big dreams. Unless they are in our head, thought Jack.

You gotta watch when you merge...

The drill sergeant had disappeared. He was content with his mission telling people off way ahead of himself. Like those white lying children conceptually taught how to act and talk. But the way Jack saw it now made it seem as if it were their own demise.

A mile down the road, the red bike was upside down. Flat tire.

Jack didn't feel any satisfaction. He was just stunned by the way things worked out when he said nothing. When he accepted it all with no remorse.

The drill sergeant hung his head down fixing a blown tire.

Jack was on his way to Sellwood. To by a pound of ground lamb. And two onions. Lamb was twice as expensive as beef. But Jack loved its flavor.

At the register he discovered his wallet was gone.

He had to ride all the way back past the drill sergeant still fixing a blown tire.

It's really funny the way things work, thought Jack again.

On the bright side, it was a good work out. He could have used his old Subaru, whose front wheels were to fall off any time soon. But he saved it for a rainy day.

What was wrong with biking twice to Sellwood, anyway?

The spring birds were chirping happy, the sky cleared up, the vision was big, and the drill sergeant was still silent fixing a tire...

Jack's Why

THE DEAL

Jack wrote a book.

It is a real-life 5D model of cultural dimensions, an intercontinental *friction* leading to a stellar *non-friction*. A real journey through the thorns of life to a knowledge of no return...

It is about deadening accommodation, self-regulation, instant gratification, and a throbbing impatience that stems from it.

Jack thinks that nowadays people seem to want to instantly get out of the way whatever is between them and their goals, as their everyday life is gradually transformed into bumps in the road to a better tomorrow that hardly ever comes.

In many cases the death knocks on their door often as an unexpected break from life. One can only find a consolation in experiencing it as a portal to *higher* and *better* dimensions.

Jack firmly believes that one might rightly refuse all deference to inherited positions, but there are a few rules to follow, if we want to run on happiness:

If we want knowledge, we ought to travel to it.

It provides constructive preventive possibilities, but it can also create new dilemmas. Once attained, there is no return, no exchange policy on it.

If we want love, it's like a flower.

Its seeds require the catalytic action of water to release hotness.

If we want freedom, we need freedom from vanity and pretentiousness first.

If we want a trip to Heaven, we should have a good night sleep before we die. We don't want to get there drained and tired. The same common mistake we would avoid going on our honeymoon…

Jack thinks those who can't catch themselves living lies should read it, particularly if they have a high respect for social climbing and wealth.

In other words—if they attach value to something for its power to indicate higher social or moral standards for self-regulation.

Jack gives them a bit of a warning, in case they expected a how-to-win-the-Powerball:

This is not a guide to teach you how to get rich quickly—*it won't make you rich at all!*

Materially, that is. Spiritually, maybe, depending on the amount of deadening accommodation and disavowed rage…

So, what's the deal?

There is no deal.

Living on three different continents and learning how to become more unobtrusive, if less harmonious, by fitting different culture norms, I have reached the peak of a mountain of my choice.

After I share this particular 360-degree view with you, it's all downhill for me, which doesn't mean you are to come along and take the brunt of all the seeded moguls on the descent.

Making it down, the trail may be too steep and narrow for grooming, and you are to follow the troughs. It will prevent you from too much momentum-building and getting out of hand, without feeling stuck in enacting patterns of compliance and defiance.

May you continue wherever it takes you, as long as it's truly yours—the journey.

If not, then maybe this book will help you get back on the path of truth.

For the price of latte, or a gallon of gas, you'll be driven from many different A's to B's that you have never considered before.

Enjoy the ride, and don't say you weren't warned...

INNUENDO

After seven CD's and four and a half books (I don't count one in since it's been scammed into a ten year contract), and also the fact that in two and a half years I'll be fifty, I started feeling a bit like:

Hello, what's going on here?

I started convincing myself that I shouldn't question God's timing and that *He* surely knows when the time is ripe for a breakthrough.

I was consoled with the usual—happy to have a roof over my head, some food, good health (I don't see doctors much since I don't have a medical insurance and God only knows what hides *under the hood*). I also have time to bike around, and *time is money* as many people don't have enough of it on their hands...

Then I started receiving e-mails about publishing on Kindle.

Cool, I thought, I have two books there, one copy sold *(that I know of)*, and maybe they are sending me some good news!

They were not bad, and personal, but they were not necessarily good either.

How to get published on Kindle and get paid at the same time...

They made me question everything from my titles to the niche and genre until I was brought down to my knees:

Is anyone going to buy it?

As they went on about three mega niches and non-fiction, I felt like I read a good joke, or a bulletin issued by *Ultimum Desideratum.*

Relationships, money, and *health* is what sells best.

Come on, guys, *seriously,* what's with *that!*

But it wasn't a joke. I was guided to check the top 100 sales on Kindle, which never occurred to me before, and there I was in for a *biggie.* It actually made me feel sad as if *Atlantis* sunk again, or something.

I mean, *what people read?*

It reminded me of that movie *What Women Want,* and all *Mel Gibson* had put himself through in vain until he heard a *little* voice.

I haven't heard any voices, I was just plain fed up.

They rake money in on how to fix this and that, how to lose weight, how to get your boyfriend back, how to make some quick money in no time—it all sounded like: *Someone pay my bills so I can do what I want,* which also is kind of disappointing: *how* people actually spend their free time.

Fiction was even worse.

50 shades of gray about a savvy rich guy and an impromptu sexy girl, chasing their own tails, or something—*who cares?*

Apparently, many people do. They're intrigued.

So, what then *intrigues* people?

First, let's check what an intrigue is:

The secret planning of something illicit or detrimental to someone.

Wow, *that* sounds interesting. It explains it all in the end.

Everything is wrong!

A *big* voice inside of me has imploded.

They should teach them how *not* to lose their boyfriends, how *not* to eat junk food and medication that makes them sick and obese.

That would imply further connotation of discipline in order not to get ill and brainwashed in the first place which, of course, means changing their lifestyles and the way they think.

As you can see, the yarn keeps unfolding and tangling towards its source.

And what is the source of a ball of yarn?

This is where *they* jump in with a new title *How To Wind a Ball Of Yarn.*

There you figure out that the very source of *it* is the very end of *it.*

To wind a new ball, you take the *end* of your yarn and hold it around your index finger. Then you gently start wrapping it around your index *and* your middle finger, and the rest is *history.*

In a way it's how it goes.

A beginning starts from an end.

Therefore I first changed the title of this book called *Tooth Bus (Greetings from the Lower Rungs)* into *Life: Bring it on and let us get it over and done with!* The way your attitude and your expectations unfold. You want everything at the drop of a hat, and you don't want to leave any money on the table. You want it all. The cake and eat it too.

Well, you can have *mine* then.

Bon appétit!

Jesus asked you to leave everything behind and follow *Him,* but you think that's a bit overrated and, *frankly,* you're a bit sick and tired of having *Jesus* shoved down you throat on regular basis.

You'd rather sport some freakish attire and wonder why Chinese babies don't smile.

For that you are to put your favorite costume on, get your ass over there, and *see it for yourself!*

There's another fact that made me write this book—even if it doesn't sell, because God broke me to make me a few times already: *nothing new on the western front*—another Google fact...

While writing it I needed to check whether I should say *a golden cycle* or *a golden circle.*

I stumbled upon the whole *philosophy* that makes this modern world spinning and spewing.

Simon Sinek's *Why, How, What.*

By learning to identify when you were living your Why and the circumstances and people that were present during those times, you will uncover the keys to discovering and articulating your personal Why.

According to him:

The Cone is a 3-dimensional representation of the Golden Circle (i.e. the Golden Circle being the top-down view). It illustrates how the levels of the Golden Circle exist inside an organization.

The top of the Cone represents the Why, the middle of the Cone represents the How and the bottom of the Cone represents the What level.

This view helps us understand the flow of information through an organization and the relative roles and responsibilities. For example, those that operate at the top of an organization are responsible for keeping the Why clear. Those in the middle of the organization are responsible for figuring out how to advance the Why and those at the What level are responsible for delivering the tangible goods—the products and services.

For an organization to operate at its maximum potential it must function like a cone...like a megaphone. That is to say, for the megaphone to work properly it must be loud and clear. Volume represents the amount of publicity or goods and services sold and clarity represents how well all those things are connected to the Why.

Well, it seems I have done something right here with my previous title—I started from the bottom, from the What level, sending greetings from Lower Rungs, delivering the tangible goods, which, in this case, is a little play on words, because the goods are digital, but not tangible.

It's another reason why I write this book. There's too much shit going on wrapped in inviting packages.

Even this title—it's a pure irony that stems out of *the tension and complexities of our contemporary society.*

Of course one wants to live forever!

But one also, sick and tired of the ruling bureaucratic inertia, wants to get it over with and *move on.* People's *Why* is not clear anymore. They're so used to moving on like hamsters in wheels.

The Sinek's *Split* has been occurring times and times again, *as stress goes up and passion goes down;* many people have become disconnected from a clear sense of *Why.*

No wonder it takes *a loud and clear megaphone, for an organization to operate at its maximum potential,* making fated galliot rowers believe *they do what they like, and like what they do,* while rowing in sync with the drum beat that gradually becomes their *Why.*

What is my *Why* then? Do I have an unquenchable purpose?

MY WHY

It's been brewing inside of me over the years.

I always had a clear sense of it, traveling across the seven seas to find it.

Ideš na kraj svijeta da nadješ bajnu djevu, my merchant marine friend Mića teased me.

Going to the end of the world to meet a charming lady...

He had already got lucky right where he was born.

I was to reach a completely diametrical opposite, as if I had dug a tunnel emerging on the other side of the world.

I took a freight *blue train* across it, all along digging a tunnel inside my heart until I emerged like a thrust spear at its other end.

Many went to seek their fortune where the money was, I went to find my true love, like a knight without a horse.

I also found out how far west I could go before east begins.

It turned out I went to *the end of the world to bring the knowledge back home,* as my grandma used to say.

It was a knowledge of no return.

No exchange policy.

I was to carry it within wherever I go, like the shadow of my inner glow.

There is ever more of it to travel to for those who seek, *quos agitat mundi labor.*

Because one cannot prevent life. It happens in unexpected ways.

It comes *at* us like an unfolding *TP* roll of the white line on the road.

When it's solid, it helps us stay on it at night, or in bad weather. When it's broken, it marks the center of the road. As it lengthens and the gaps shorten, it means there is a hazard ahead. Dealing with it is up to *us*. But not always...

First time I thought I had reached the end of the world was in Bretagne, the west coast of France. Like a pre-Columbian pilgrim, I stared at the line of horizon dividing the sky from the ocean as if they were *just* two big shades of gray.

The second time I was on a bus to Galway, the west coast of Ireland.

After a thirty-hour journey, crossing the Irish sea by ferry (one bearded guy woke me up, cursing like a pirate, requesting his spot on the floor back), and then busing across the country, I thought *this* had to be *it*, because it felt like it.

Already in Manchester, 5 a.m., the Irish proletarians boarded the bus cracking their beers open, lighting their cigarettes, and yelling at the three *French Female Frogs* in the back to *shut it!*

It's only a few years later, as I boarded a plane that took me over the big pond, that I reached the far west in Oregon, and then, after crossing the *International Date Line,* I woke up in the far east, still going west. Until I had reached the Indian Ocean.

The Australian sun shone like a ducat.

If I kept going, I'd have found myself in Africa, not *that* far from where I had started.

I took a rain check on it, even though *the game* wasn't rained out.

I was tired needing to take a load off.

My *easting value* had spun me out. Following the *Universal Transverse Mercator* system, my *east-western* origin was placed way west of the *central meridian*, now referred to as the zone's *false origin*.

All I knew was that I came from Sarajevo, *where east offered to shake hands, but west didn't accept it.*

One called it *a geographical metaphor of a failed meeting.*

Some would say *we did our part,* the same as a transverse wave *naturally* transports energy from east to west, or transverse ranges run the same way.

So had I also followed the same transversal line carried more by eastern winds, although I nursed both sides within, being born to it as well as adapting to it daily.

For example, at school we were taught Cyrillic *and* Latin alphabet of 30 letters each, which became our second nature.

Brought up with more passive behaviors when interacting with adults, we were less willing to ask for extra help or to admit what we didn't understand, as opposed to those whose aggressive attitude came from more driven and ambitious places.

It was a fertile loam for growing preconceived notions and nursing false audacities easily made, but everyone's unique background was valued.

Perhaps it was not the only place on earth where four biggest religions crossed their paths within 500 square feet, but it definitely was the only place where Marxism also flourished, and thus Jesus' teachings and ideology ironically appeared closer to Communism than Capitalism.

But hardly anyone offered prayers to *the quarters of the four winds,* as the Mongols did.

The main characteristic of far east, notably high Asia, in the time of Genghis Khan, were:

An oath of comradeship was more binding then the pledge of a king.

Scythians, as the Greeks called them, were nomads sticking to their determination, which was not a matter of false pride. They had little use for weak characters. Retribution was an obligation. One of their wise counselors once said:

If we begin to build towns and change our old habits, we shall not prosper. Besides, monasteries and temples breed mildness of character, and it is only the fierce and warlike who dominate mankind.

Frederick II of Germany wrote to Henry III of England that *the "Tatars" must be no less than the punishment of God, visited upon Christendom for its sins, and the Tatars themselves the descendants of the missing ten tribes of Israel who had worshiped the golden calf and had been penned up for their idolatry within the wastes of Asia.*

The reason why I mention all this is to distinguish the *Why* of the greatest conqueror on the planet Earth emerging from the Gobi desert.

A nomad, a hunter and herder of beasts, outgeneraled the powers of three empires; a barbarian who had never seen a city and did not know the use of writing drew up a code of laws for fifty peoples.

It's pretty much self-explanatory. No *writing,* no *monasteries,* and no *cities.*

Jerusalem, Athens, Rome, and London together couldn't stop him.

The pillars of conservatism in a nut-shell that, therefore, thrived *here,* starting in Philadelphia, introducing *the freedom to allocate your own resources in a free market* and *pursue virtue.*

A far cry from the short but powerful verbal portrait of Genghis:

Being a Mongol, he wanted only what he needed.

Bear that in mind, if today, according to speech doctors, *your words are the portrait of your success.* It's totally opposite to Temujin's speaking very little *only after meditating on what he would say.*

Now they teach you that *when you learn to express yourself and master the art of painting the verbal portrait, you will have a leadership skill for life.*

The same technique was used by traveling medicine shows putting on performances while peddling miracle cures and elixirs of dubious nature.

The latest DNA research revealed that *genetic markers linking people living in the Russian republic of Altai, southern Siberia, with indigenous populations in North America.*

Roughly 20-25,000 years ago, these prehistoric humans carried their Asian genetic lineages up into the far reaches of Siberia and eventually across the then-exposed Bering land mass into the Americas.

Isn't it ironic that eventually some of the Temujin's bloodline, *the Ural-Altaic race,* had crossed *Beringia,* settling down in this vast land simply calling themselves *People,* or *the flesh,* and then centuries later welcomed the infestation of white westerners coming from east?

En fin, bref, as the French would say...

My *Why,* instead of My *Way,* apart from finding a charming lady, is still *offering to shake hands with west* that *doesn't accept it.*

Whether I came across Atlantic or Pacific pond, my unquenchable purpose is to make them see and feel the *drastic difference,* but their eyes are glazed over with a predictable triple 8 boredom dreaming about the *A-List* stardom.

8 hours of sleep, 8 hours of work, 8 hours of leisure time.

Working mostly overtime, they probably couldn't care less about *Numerology* that says:

Totaled the letters that make up Jesus' Name in Greek come to 888!

It's overrated! Or underestimated.

Because, think deeper, if triple 8 denotes the divine dimension, there goes their *stardom.*

But it's not the one they're after...

They are just *bored shitless,* as some rehab residents explain their reasons.

Oh, of course, we do shake hands often simply introducing each other!

Even then they withdraw them quickly as if they have touched a jelly fish.

Sometimes I have an urge to squeeze them and not let go for a few seconds longer, just for fun (now *that* would seem *weird),* since there is still a lack of trust on their part that is subconsciously directed toward themselves first.

More and more they are aware of their wrong doing, but they just don't know any better. They are mainly taught *what* to think instead of *how.* Thus they are perfectly suited for the bottom of *the Cone,* representing *What.*

They have a *Why* that is overwhelming and overbearing at times. Maybe therefore one often finds them on top of the game, for the same reasons young Temujin became a Khan:

Physical prowess he had, and watchfulness, and a growing wisdom kept the nucleus of a clan about him.

The only big difference is that clans are left way back in Scotland, or it just appears so.

Maybe there is *a* clan that *wags the dog* behind the curtains somewhere over the rainbow.

One of them, McDonald's, has definitely spread around the world.

As far as the east is from the west...

IMPLODING

Auckland, New Zealand, 1999.

Bursting inwardly…

I have been groping for a right word to enlighten my spirit for days now, trying to express the shape I am in. I have been writing this book in my head on and on. Even this morning I had a few pages ready for printing (in my head, of course).

Particularly this morning, for yesterday I've hit the bottom again. A very familiar bottom so well known to me that it seemed like a part of my life. Something I can count on. Something that never fails, always waiting there for me like a concrete floor. I can put my bewildered feet on it and watch them grow into the ground.

Pour some hard rain on me, *Dear God,* and the tulips will start blossoming forced out of my ears. The floor is made of concrete, but my ribs are of *dirt,* and I am sure they both will find a *common ground.* A higher one even, like in the Holy Book.

But in the *Real Book,* written by a mortal carnation, it says: *Implosion.*

It says: *Bursting inwardly.*

Who else but *Dear Henry* could think of a better way to describe something so vivid and divine? One maybe cannot explode literally. For one reason or another one *should not* explode. It would cause a general confusion.

One is to be concerned about the world—this world and its reasons as well as its excuses. Hence one is free to implode. No picture shows, no tickets to buy, no dressed gorillas to watch the endless lines of items ever waiting to get in. No empty smiles and busy catwalks. Just a soundless and speechless radiation of the heart reaching out for the seventh heaven floor…

Meanwhile, as the concrete floor waits for my fall and hit, I have wound up in that ridiculous position again. Sitting on a bench of an airport with all my stuff piled up on a little trolley.

If I keep watching my feet grow into the ground, if only for a second longer I keep thinking about my troubled life, then my *other* life, the one on the little trolley, starts drifting off like a rollaway bed.

I think your trolley is about to hit the road, noticed a woman sitting on the same bench.

She tried to sound impersonal and funny at the same time.

Never get too friendly…

I always remember that incident at the *Temple,* in the Queen Street, when the bartender Tim started behaving as if he had a share in my life insurance policy.

Don't know what's wrong with him, said I to Pule, *obviously I'm too friendly…*

As it turned out, I have said it out too loud, not fighting a natural urge to fill the room with constant sound. Tim had heard it and started snapping at me in that strange Anglo-Kiwi fashion. Boneless and spineless.

Rupp explained it well: *They're insecure* (talking about Aussies and Kiwis).

I would also add they are *primitive*. Being insecure doesn't give you the right to be rude. It stems from the ancient Anglo-Saxon fog. It's how they conquered half of the world. They may call it *diplomacy,* but it's a pure backstabbing. And it still works. They get what they are after, *in the end.* Whether it is a piece of land, a country, or a whole continent. Half of the world speaks English, and there must be a valid reason for it.

On the concrete floor, my both lives—the imagined one and the one on the little trolley—have met again.

I moved out of my windowless room above the *Femme Fatale,* in the Wellesley Street, packed everything up, drove all the way to *Onehunga* to say goodbye to Lucas (he was not home as usual), and then to *Howick* to park my old *Subaru Leone* in Pule's garden. Then he and Bridget drove me, and all my stuff, to the Auckland International Airport. Everything was organized the way Germans would do. Just one dent in it. With ordinary human beings there is always that one thing they either forget about or do not think of…

The school holidays.

How in the world could I have forgotten about them damn school holidays?

I thought of it just a few days before…

I even talked about it.

Cindy, my wife, could have been here as her kids had suddenly decided to spend their holidays with their father Sean. My name is Jack, by the way.

Had we talked *less* on the phone, my wife could have gotten the $1000 ticket to fly over from Perth. But then again, three months ago, she flew from Auckland to Perth…

It's when I start watching my motionless feet grow into a concrete floor, while my other life, the one on the little trolley *is about to hit the road.* It's already the fifth time this year I've been sitting on probably the very same bench and the only *real thing,* heavy at that, is my life on a little trolley. A huge army duffle bag, a medium, and a little one, *and a guitar.*

Lucky I didn't bring the amplifier. Not only they required my attention, I was also to *carry* them as a load, *My Dear Lord,* for fifteen years now. Fifteen long years, and I won't even tell you where I was born and what all had happened since I left home. Just last couple of years is enough. Otherwise, I get too dizzy, and then something clicks in my head.

Now, as I think about what I have just said, I should still mention a few other things in order for you to understand better my leave-taking and why I sit at the Auckland International Airport, and not another one, although any would do…

This one is the most familiar, together with the one in Portland, Oregon. It's where my parents live (not together, though), and it's where I was headed to. For the same reason I did in August last year.

My father had issues with his *bug,* but another big news was my mother proposed him to re-marry her. Odd enough to put it that way. Let's say she wanted to give it a go one more time for the sake of us kids to stop our continent hopping. Only to find out *again* the same reason why she ever left him.

Nothing without love, my son, she concluded, *real love.*

In his funny way, my father really loved her, but it didn't seem real enough to her.

It broke my heart kissing my parents goodbye, leaving them behind in a big land of plastic dreams and wide-open spaces. The funny thing is my father would become a *Citizen* this year without being able to pledge because of his broken English. In fact, it is not even broken. There is hardly anything breakable about it. He gets by upon his big smile, like in that *Wild World* song, or by just being a mean and grumpy old bugger.

My mother is different. While in France, she learned some French, and now in the States her English is better than what most of the Mexicans speak. Her spirits are always high simply believing in God and love.

Once I had phoned her because a high blood pressure in my head gave me a fright and I wanted to hear a familiar voice. Cindy was at work, and it was too late to call my sister being in a different time zone.

Like any old son, I called my mother. I also had not heard from her for a few weeks. As soon as I mentioned headache and dizziness, the tone of her voice changed and it sounded as if God himself spoke to me, or at least one of the archangels or priests, although I shouldn't compare *Him* with anybody. In most cases it is a poor comparison. Let us say her voice sounded definite:

Just imagine you are all alone in this world…

Recalling it better now, I desperately needed to hear the voice of someone that knew me well. I had a feeling I was dying somewhere *Down Under,* far from everything I was used to, and no one was even able to identify me. I swallowed my tears choking on them. It's always good to the come to an end, reaching the bottom. Then there is no more suffering. It's where it stops.

Imagine you are all alone in this world…'cause, in the end, you are. And if you are to die, put a smile on your face. Remember the good things. The happy moments, if there were any. Just one is enough. There must have been one.

Right now the *Sky Tower* is shining purple in the night. It looks like an unreal injection from a heroin addict's dream. It's piercing the darkness like a crazy rocket on the top of a hill, standing still like an illusion. Yet strong enough to tear apart today's black heavy clouds. It seemed as if it was going to rain for forty nights and days straight.

But now the pressure is gone. One can breathe again. The rain has washed the streets clean. It is unusually calm for a Friday's big night out. The music has stopped and only a few cars break the silence *tous les temps en temps.* After midnight some children are still drunk. Soon they'll be back home with their ordinary pangs and frustrations. Once a week they let it out of their system so they could be good kids until the next Friday. It is sad to realize that drugs and alcohol are their only weapon in an eternal battle with Insecurity.

I feel better again. The heavy clouds are gone, the sun is high. The last two days I felt trapped. It was hard enough for me to pack up and leave again. I hesitated too long. As I finally moved on, a blonde shark behind the counter cut me in two with a pair of ice cold blue eyes:

The school holidays are starting tomorrow and we are fully booked for the next few days. We had already taken three people off the plane.

My hands still trembled from carrying a heavy load. I desperately tried to find a *companion-limited-write-your-own-pleasure-travel-ticket* that I had already signed. My sister gave me four last time she was here. It was only two weeks ago and I had better left with her, but I was hesitating again.

Was I going to transfer the New Zealand work visa from my old passport to the new one? Or was I going to leave it blank and wait for the mighty decision of the Australian immigration?

It's been that way since I was asked to leave, July 14, the *Bastille Day*. I was sitting in a west Australian county jail, a beautiful day it was. I could see the crisp blue sky between the bars on the ceiling. A seagull swam free along them as if in a perfectly clear and bottomless swimming pool. I was politely told I was going to be held there till an evening plane would take me to the *Detention Center* in Perth, but still: never in my life behind the bars, let alone on the ceiling, and I was scared.

The floor was spat on and chewed up though I was lucky they put me in the *garden*. The cells looked like concrete microwave ovens. Naked floors and unbreakable polycarbonate windows.

Once they shut you in, there is no even good old iron bars to squeeze and hold on to. Except for those on the garden's *ceiling*. I could not reach them, but I could still see the sky.

The almighty blue sky, always there, warm and deep like a soul. It felt like a nice place to be at the end of a lifelong journey.

DOWN UNDER

Perhaps the most thrilling and outstanding situation is having two opposites together: power and no power, electricity and no electricity, rich and poor, beautiful and ugly, love and hate…

At this moment there are several extraordinary circumstances.

One of them is that I'm in Australia.

The other one is that I'm in a suburb called Dee Why.

The most amazing one is that I live in the place with no electricity and use *PowerBook G4* to write about it. I don't even know how much time I have left before the battery runs out. I can bring it to one of the little Internet cafés and recharge it while I check my email, get a few more hours of power, and get back to creating a masterpiece. But they already are created, like *Electricity*.

If one wants to write in the candlelight, then use a typewriter: another 100 or 200 years old miracle.

The mother masterpiece of them all is a break of dawn.

It is why, for centuries, stories had been told, waiting for the daylight to come back again, worshiped and glorious.

To feel even more medieval, I'm surrounded by some real wildlife here as well.

Right now some birds called rainbow lorikeets are chirping like mad. Of course, they are mesmerizing, but, at night, it's another story. At dusk, as the sun melts into a pitch dark, they come, one by one, straight from the top, as if they lived in another world during the day, and one wonders *where?*

Possums are almost like raccoons, but their eyes are more bulgy, as if they had problems with their thyroid glands. They seemed ready to scream and scratch one's eyes out at any given moment. Isn't it uncanny that some women have the similar features?

One could be sitting tired and thoughtful after dusk, after a finished day of work, or a plate of meat, a bottle of drink, a cigarette, or a pleasant and unpleasant thought often following each other. Then, right in front of you, crossing over a gum tree branch, they come like a fearless night squad. The creatures of the dark, one by one, or one on top of the other, a mother and a child.

Oldwin says they sometimes try to get rid of their kids, shaking them off their back, but in vain, because they hold on tight to their mother's fur, thus they both keep going, in quest for food. After a few *Wild Turkeys* with *Coke* that put him in a good mood, Oldwin would reach out with his long arm, offering them some bread.

He also uses a flashlight, if it happened to be around, and then, like in cartoons, one can see their eyes, on top of each other, staring at you without blinking. In front of them there's bread and a couple of strangers, but the hunger makes them fearless, and it's where a cartoon evolves into the *Discovery* channel. It also parallels a stand-up comedy, where tipsy Owen teases them, calling them names, and they become the audience, curiously watching him trying to be funny and bitter at the same time.

A few weeks later the electricity is back! But, it is another place, another face. It's still Dee Why, *estamos en el culo del mundo,* on the top of a hill. Kay Road, 36, at Pavo's.

What happened to Oldwin? Is he still in the world of darkness?

Maybe he moved, maybe not yet...

I talked to him the day before yesterday and he was still there. Went to the court, electricity was still not paid, the rent either. The people with long wigs told him he's got to move out, so they probably have set a date too.

I left that day. At first I was going to do it like a camel in *omnia mea mecum porte* style. The suitcase was bursting out with clothes not worn once, but it had wheels. On top of it another duffle bag, two little backpacks, three jackets, sleeping bag, and a guitar in the left hand. I pushed it up and down across the room to get the picture, to get the feel of it. It was heavy. Maybe I could have dragged it across the Dee Why, but the Kay Road and the top of the hill would have taken their toll.

If Oldwin had only let me cut a spare key, but he was funny about it. I felt like some kind of a prisoner. He wouldn't answer the phone, he wouldn't answer the door either. I had to knock and knock till he'd appear out of the dark silence, acting strange.

Other than that, he helped me with a few days of work. I made $500 without paying the rent for two weeks. I really appreciated it and it was hard for me to leave, but there was no price for freedom. Feeling free to come and go, having your own key, and not having your heart in your throat all the time—*what if he doesn't open the door?*

What if I can't even get to the pile of stuff I carry around the world like a *Sherpa* (saucepan, in my language)? A guitar, laptop, camera, CD's with music and photos, moleskins, notes, papers, stupid clothes...

What would I have for the police—you know, officer, I was here with this guy, living in the dark, I met him in Avalon while we were all trying to move into that 5 bedroom mansion in Cove Street, and for the time being he offered me a place to stay and some work too (although he often acted like a drill sergeant), *and now he's not there!*

Maybe I have become a little paranoid after all the years of compiling *The New Histories* that not many cared about. Like a hobo riding the gusty bus, without accounting for taste, completely depending on somebody's goodwill, or not at all—both cases had their ups and downs—I developed a need for minimal safety. A little door with a little key that works, so that I can think about other things in life. Not to mention creation, inspiration *and* aspiration. I mean, little things like breathe the air, get the weight off the chest, and so on.

And there I was, living without electricity with the drill sergeant Oldwin.

He actually left the US Navy some fifteen years ago, after he met Claire in Sydney, and some fifteen years later she left with three little boys, his name on the lease, with all bills to pay, and a nightmare to tame.

As he was and is an amazing handy man, a soldier at heart, I mean, he really likes his job and does it well, he maintained *that* side of sanity pretty well. The emotional one was drowning in the amber sea of *Wild Turkey* mixed with *Coca-Cola* and occasional river of *Victoria Bitter*. Only his eyes remained blue, deep blue as the Ocean that pounds the rocks around this sleepy continent. When he drank he'd become amazingly childlike, his heart would open, but sober he was as bitter and acid as the Australian beer.

Is it because he was brought up in the American way: suppressed emotions, tough & sarcastic, but still a child, a dad that needs a father? Then what's the difference between the American and Australian Spirit? Handicapped souls but perfect machines still operating: an amazing variety of similar problems.

It all stems from a small town *Childhood*. Rigid upbringing to toughen one up, but also to eliminate the spectrum of emotions and channel it into a productive stream of a few values—work, keep busy, mind your own business, and maintain sanity within insanity.

I was getting used to living without electricity, only gas, Sunrise instead of Sunset, wild birds' chirping in the morning while saluting life, facing a constant loneliness on the outside. Everybody busy and lonely, attached to their mobile phones, expecting a call out of blue, a miraculous number to ring like a *Powerball*. The kids pampered in a distant English way, kept on a short leash within exercised emotions...

Me, crucified between longing for my family and keeping the residency here up and running, at the same time trained to live within the minimal conditions (again TV is out of the picture). The life becomes more vivid and simple, basic but meaningful, reading in the candlelight, every sentence remains carved deep into the memory, as an eternal imprint, the brain using its own technology, not digital but emotional...

––––––––––

Australia is isolated on a huge island, its sky crystal blue, the dirt red, yellow and white. Many people show no genuine joy, only a self-fulfilling presence. It is a paradise for birds and insects. Abandoned by the spirit human bodies lie on the beaches like empty carcasses trained to provide and relax weekly, to pay the bills and get drunk on Friday, and keep going with plans *B* stashed at the back of a general mind...

I wrote a few lines by candlelight, and then walked down the street to phone George, 4 a.m. his time. It was snowing in Suisse, he had just watched *Dr. Zhivago*, had a couple of bottles of wine, talking about the best love as unrequited, followed only half way and then left floating...his wife and kids asleep... Me, talking about how tired I was from roaming around the world, not knowing how long I would last here. He recommended me to stay, *drop the anchor, bite the bullet...*

Then I called home (I call it *home* because my whole family is there, in America) trying to get through to talk to little Michael before they leave again.

He's the only one saying my name every day no matter what, he got used to me, can hardly put a sentence together, but most of it is inspired by the things we did together, as I carried him around every time he reached out with his little arms, feeling safe, having me like some sort of wheels. *Tut, tut!* A freight train passing by, and we run out on the balcony to wave.

Little simple things…

Huge waves were pounding the beach, the remnants of the cyclone Larry, or Wati. I sat on a sunlit bench for a while and talked to a 81-year-old from *Korčula,* where Marco Polo was born.

The old man came here 40 years ago, starting from scratch working in hotels, pretending he knew English well…

The ocean was amazing, the shear force of the Universe, everybody watching a free entertainment. The surfers looked like helpless mosquitoes floating in a stirred bathtub as if a huge invisible baby played there with his rubber ducks…

Nothing looked more divine than those emerald waves elegantly crashing, rolling and unfolding like heavy green and blue blankets. White crests foamed in the wind topping off a few primitive basic comments in the background.

It was like some kind of a game: the prisoners of a virginal beauty, the people here—*what's the deal?*

They don't belong here; they should be elsewhere with their sausage roll and coke attitude, fish and chips, *whatever.*

They should be sent back, *wherever,* but one would not really want them there either, not enough room, so they're stuck here on their big island, just provide enough food and drinks, and they'll surf happily ever after…

———

Pavo is juxtaposed to Oldwin. It's a living proof how world is small and yet huge in contrasts.

Pavo is from Montenegro, also divorced, four kids—they're bigger though, and he's older too. Pavo doesn't live in darkness, he pays his bills; he's got tenants paying him rent. He rents a whole house, and he lives on the top floor like a captain on the bridge, controlling the course of his shipwreck as if stuck on a hilltop after a big flood.

He builds another castle next to this old one that he'll pull apart and build another on top of it. Pavo drinks, every night. Pavo gambles. Last night he took me to the *RSL* club full of slot machines.

The night before they wouldn't let us in because he was dead drunk, clashing with the doorman and his manager, exchanging the *F* words. Last night we got in, and I couldn't believe all those people feeding *50 dollar* bills into those funny machines that spin numbers and some cartoon like pictures of native American Indians, teepees and dream catchers.

Pavo mistook teepees for pyramids. He said we were only going to have a coffee and head back, but then he appeared a bit nervous, fidgeting. He was debating whether to sit behind one of the machines.

His workmate Stipe was there too, sipping on a light beer, but not playing. Originally from around Zadar, came here 1969.

Pavo and him work together, maintaining a huge property for a rich guy Milan. Back in Serbia a whole plant was built on his father's land, and he was only offered a job for it, so he escaped, and came here, cutting the sugar cane, and afterwards becoming one of the richest people in the area. Pavo's father's forests were *also taken by partisans*, as he says. Now he takes care of Milan's property.

I'm here, sharing his big room with him, listening to him snore, greeting the sunrise we're surrounded by every morning. The entire corner around my bed is a big window.

Last night I gave Pavo 140$ and couldn't believe how fast that machine swallowed the money. A week's rent. We could have done many things with it. As I looked around every one was into it. Money, making and wasting it, and the machines never stopped. The government made sure everything worked just fine. It even organized the courses to cure the addiction, as it kept going viral.

Magnificent breaks of dawn, surrounded by windows, my bed in the corner of the room facing east. Every morning pink little clouds stretch across the blue skies as the sun rises.

Stipe comes in to wake Pavo up, always with a little comment *(still sleeping?)*, because Stipe is a stoic and Pavo drinks and gambles, but they both go together to do the same work ensuring the proper functioning of Milan's property.

It's a Pavo-Stipe paradigm that resembles a time warp: the crucial difference between Serbs and Croats, mysteriously suspending the passage of time every half a century, like two plates clashing, pulling apart, or sliding past each other parallel to their shared boundaries, with a constant pushing action along the border between them.

Pavo is a hard working man from Montenegro, (some might scrunch their eyebrows in wonder after all the jokes about them being lazy), but he also lives with a notion that nothing lasts forever, ready not to wake up the next morning, living for the moment, still stingy a bit, as opposed to Stipe going to bed early, not drinking, smoking or gambling, considering Pavo *a lost case,* while being his prudent and frugal tenant...

He deems romantic the ways Pavo falls prey to pride as long as he doesn't clash with his shocking Capricorn's realism. Stipe then throws up his hands abandoning the power-struggle scene realizing that Pavo only pretends being manipulated by the others to be accepted, seeming as if he had been acting out absurd instructions. The thing is, he is set in his ways passed on from one generation to the next, and he rarely allows his traditional vision any scope.

In all that I'm still looking for work, longing for my family, literally dwelling between Pavo and Stipe, and listening to their stories. They're both divorced, their parents dead, as they enter into their sixties finding themselves alone.

Kiro, the Macedonian hairdresser, my age, also divorced twice, is thinking of going back home, opening boutiques and breeding rabbits and canaries in Skopje.

I visited him yesterday in the barbershop, where he works for *Gino the Italian*. As if in an old movie, it was surrounded by small streets and laneways, where everybody knew everybody except they were different nationalities developing their own characters, and it still didn't feel like home.

Kiro and I speak our languages, and Gino doesn't understand any of it.

Kiro also feels a little exploited, working long hours for little money, buying second hand stuff, packing a whole container to send back home, whereas Gino, like an old spider, sits in his shop all day, waiting for *the kill* to walk in.

Yesterday Pavo had some wine *(the fruity lexia)* that we went to get for him. He said the 5-liter cask had *a picture of a horse on it*, but we couldn't find it. The funny scene in the bottle shop was explaining it to the shopkeeper:

We're after a wine, you know, the one with a horse on it...

He looked at us crossways as if we were a couple of dumb foreigners not knowing exactly what we were talking about.

Kiro also cut my hair, since my little trimmer died. He borrowed one from work, and Gino wasn't very happy. His Calabrian sideburns stood the test of time for the last fifty years, together with their attitude before World War II…and after as well.

―――――――

I blew my gig with Oldwin yesterday. He gave it to somebody else because there was a misunderstanding sms-ing him. First he said there was work, and to meet him at 27 Harbord Road at 6.30 a.m. I didn't have enough credit to call him back so I sent the message I'd be at his place the following night, to discuss it.

I couldn't really write a long message either because my hands were full of shopping bags climbing up the Kay Road, and I also didn't know what was going to happen yesterday since I had to start doing sales with an audio company in Warrywood.

Pavo dropped me off there at 7.30 in the morning and showed me around

The land was initially owned by our people, he said, *but then gradually sold to various companies.*

The street where I got off was called Vuko place. It strangely felt like *chez nous.*

The sales people had a typical hustling attitude. On the wall there were various paroles like *winners make things happen, losers let things happen,* and basically it was: you go out and sell the stuff with a right attitude, which means you are to put a biggest lying smile on your face and talk to everybody like they're your loving family—and ask them to pay cash only.

Then they came in, the young hustlers in their twenties, all hangover after the Easter holidays, but acting as if the adrenalin was gushing out of their ears: *this week they'll sell at least fifteen home theater surrounding systems each!*

Yeah, go for it boys!

The boss was a slim Dutchman creating *we can do it* atmosphere, believing one did the same thing in the States. I still thought we were going out with a van full of speakers to park somewhere and stop the people in the street. My trainer Kieff already started with a territorial attitude, and deep inside I was so happy to be past that stage in life. Every time I realized more and more people were prisoners of their own minds.

He was a real *go-for-it* sort of Brad Pitt from the movie *Kalifornia,* a little more sophisticated, thank God. Plus, he was proud of his hangover farts, grinning manly about their nastiness.

I felt like on a mission, thinking to myself: if you want to write a book like Herodotus did, and call it *The New Histories,* or something, *you are to put up with it.* It's amazing how one can actually do anything when reasons are justified by any valid measure or opinion…

The both windows were rolled down, but not for farts. Kieff first asked me, in a street-smart manner, *what sort of work I did?*

I said I was forty, did this and that. He only wanted to know if I could drive, handing me the keys.

There I was, after a couple of weeks not driving—Rachel and I drove up to *Noosa*, in a new automatic *Hyundai Elantra,* when only I farted occasionally—hopping in a diesel van and straight into the early morning Sydney's *Rat Race.*

It would have been *OK,* but whenever I deal with an attitude that's unnecessary and destructive; whenever my antennas sense a tension of any kind of bullying nature that disharmonizes the necessary amount of balance within the Universe, it's when I have to arm myself with a little known but nonetheless glorious magnetic field discovered by Tesla, who would understand me better at least for the fact that we speak the same language, and probably share a few similar ideas...

Kieff certainly would have no idea what I'm talking about.

His only mission in life was to hustle people like some sort of a predatory green-eyed fly with the huge fake *Dior's* sunglasses that became popular thanks to *Paris Hilton* species, together with the *authentic* ball hat made famous by *Mr. Pitt* from *Kalifornia.*

The only reason why I was driving, said Kieff, *is because he lost his driver's license to speeding and all the demerit points.* He was also a wannabe race-driver.

So I drove not exactly understanding my mission until he started smiling and yelling at other people driving along, waving at them to open their windows and listen to his sick proposal, all done within the sales laws, of course:

Hey bud, d'you wanna a home theater, I got one for free?

He'd wave with a prepared shipping order, with signatures already on it, and the name *Jetro Distribution, Maxaudio.com.* People would roll their windows down thinking he needed driving directions or something.

He'd keep on with stories about home theaters that he was to get rid of dirt-cheap. If some people curiously asked *"how much?"* he'd talk them into pulling over (most of them were on their way to work) to check it out, telling them *normally it's a $3,600 sound system,* and, *buddy, how much can you get?*

I was still mesmerized by the whole thing, thinking I needed work to prove my residency intentions, but at the same time I wanted to tell those people the guy was a maniac and to just keep driving to their hopefully honest jobs.

He managed to make some of them pull over and I still couldn't believe they did. In the States nobody would, seeing a *Kalifornia Brad Pitt* smiling and waving at them. Peter, the self-fulfilled Dutchmen, proudly stood for the fact that this kind of sales were invented in the States, since the product is from there too: *Fleetwood* tower speakers and what not.

As Kieff's actions in the end proved futile, he told me to stop the car so that he can show me how the things were properly done. He was my coach, and he also complained that I kept my foot on the clutch for too long, wearing it off.

He was a better driver, originally from Adelaide, doing the same thing in Melbourne adrenalin pumped for almost 3 years. He actually had a few wise observations about how in this job *you don't really need to know your roundabouts,* and the best thing was to be lost in the crowd, just drive along like a bird of prey, targeting the right victim.

But the whole foundation was wrong. *It was schizophrenic!*

As the most of the world was, at least Kieff did his job energetically, even politely, if anybody smiled back at him. If somebody just waved back in a *keep your BS away* manner, then he'd feel a little hurt and say something impolite accompanied with a nasty fart. Then he'd feel better about himself again and keep driving like a king of the road waving at mature women.

I like older ladies, mate, there's nothing better than be a toy-boy and have a sugar mamma!

Before that he had stopped at his place to get the cigarettes. He had also forgotten to kiss his girlfriend, and then he went on with his crazy mission again as if the whole world was a secret home theater brotherhood that everybody was hooked on.

I couldn't believe what I got myself into, following *the right path* looking for work, trying to fit in and prove myself, only to juxtapose creating the feeling of being a misfit.

We drove all the way to Liverpool like madmen, stopping at every filling station. Kieff talked to guys looking like him, as well as to those that looked successful. No talking to women.

They get scared, he said, without realizing that they didn't really care about home theaters, let alone a guy waving at them from an unmarked van.

Another thing, still maintaining human conditions, I offered him a pastry I got that morning.

Pavo had stopped by the local bakery and took all the bread they didn't sell the day before, the car was packed with it. He takes it to Milan's property to feed the ducks and brings the leftovers back home.

I picked three little breads and put them in my backpack. I offered one to Kieff, as he drove madly up and down the highway 54, complaining about his hangover and *his mojo not being up and running yet.*

God, I wondered what he'd do with his mojo on!

Surprised, he accepted asking what it was.

Some kind of pastry, I don't know, *(it's a piece of bread man!),* I got it this morning at the bakery...

He ate it still driving and getting people's attention.

They couldn't understand his fast street talk with all the *buddy, champ & bro'* stuff, and probably because he looked like a cheap entertainment—*any will do during a rush hour!*

It also looked a little mysterious: a white unmarked van with a guy yelling out some free offers.

After the a piece of bread I gave him, he pulled over at the nearest gas station, and told me to wait a sec.

He carried back two bottles of orange and green *Gatorade*. Not that I'd ever buy *and* drink it, but I didn't want to become some misunderstood nuisance, *a dickhead on a stupid prick,* thus I convinced myself to accept it as a friendly gesture.

Kieff jumped back into the van, opened one bottle, I think it was green, had a few sips, and placed it into the bottle holder. The orange one reached me only for a split second, and then took a sharp right turn (or left for him) straight into a little container between us. He didn't do it to be mean or anything like it, he just did it—*it was his nature.*

That act, together with previous experiences throughout different countries, struck me surprised as always. No matter how many times it happened, it was always *as good as the first time.*

Now that I'm forty-one (when maturing is caused both by physical limitations simultaneously occurring tiresome and repetitive *and* by apparently full developing of our brain), one is to seek spiritual inspirations and thus allay fears of becoming just a *300,000-mile* engine at its best.

At times I'm amazed by the outside events, considering them as the outer elements that now affect me only as acts of God, nothing personal. 5-10 years ago I'd maybe steam out of my skin, open the door and jump out of the car while still in motion. It's called young blood.

One is to have an out of the body experience in order to see oneself from behind and notice some surprising facts. Nowadays they use cameras, so the movie stars can practice their every little move and look perfect at any age until their skin starts drying up.

Simple people can go to an elevator with a surrounding mirror, and see themselves from behind or any possible angle that's beyond their nose.

Then they go:

Oh my, look at my posture, look at my shoulders, the right is lower from the left, I'm bald…

The same goes for their souls. They look different from behind, as one refuses to look there for the reality that animates them.

Instead of being angry at Kieff, even though I still muttered a few *F* words, I accepted the fact that he, being in his twenties, still didn't see his soul at its worst. Ignorance held sway anyway, no matter what the age.

I was to remain in the van like a piece of furniture, since we had not gone through the half of the day yet. Or else, I could have gotten out in the middle of the highway, finding my way back, paying for trains and buses, seeking some genuine souls to point me in the right direction.

It seemed as if my efforts had come to naught.

I was unprepared again, hemmed in by convention, chancing upon solutions I had jumped in the river going with the flow, and it was the part of my mission. I calmed myself down:

You want to write about people and customs!

You want to show the world how nothing changed and got even worse!

There you go, *mate…*

Still, life was good. I heaved a sigh of relief thinking about the amazing sunrise that greeted us when we stepped outdoors in the morning, the pink clouds like cotton candy caressing us from above. The crazy little flocks of lorikeets jumping from tree to tree and saluting the orange red sunsets, the green and blue ocean foaming upon the golden sands…

Nobody was selling it—nobody was buying it.

The friendly bird that just landed on the old, rotten balustrade (it's to be demolished in a couple of weeks) looked at me and chirped *Hi,* taking off in a flash.

Did he hustle me, was he rude, did he beg?

Just like a bird, he was the part of the scene rolling in and out, each and every day, singing, making do with the wind and clouds. *Move it to the left, move it to the right,* it's the same old place.

Brick houses, home or *any* theaters—it's a man's job to make it and unmake it.

It's got nothing to do with the sun reflecting upon the sea on the horizon right now like liquid gold. It's enough to see it and admire it. Why would one want to touch and hold it in his hands, fumble it with his sweaty, sticky fingers?

It looks like Jesus could appear any moment, walking upon that golden water. The wall of the clouds behind is gray and heavy, but the sun has found a hole in it and now the gates are wide open. The whole ocean shines like an underwater star…

Enough of sales stories, enough of Kieff, bless his heart!

I was supposed to be back there this morning, another day driving up and down the highway, stopping at every possible gas station, pulling over, asking people for $1000 cash—*who in the world carries it around?* Or ask them to go to the nearest *ATM…*

Yet, some people do, they sold a few home theaters, somebody bought them. Maybe right now, this moment, somebody does. But here I am, at the top of the Kay Road, with no *surround system.*

I've got a surround window instead. One side looks at the Long Reef (instead of Kieff), and the other down at Manly, even the Harbor Bridge in the distance, with all the roofs of houses beneath the trees swaying in the breeze.

I know, Kieff is selling hard to own a house like this some day, and I'm in it *now*. A few roaches milling around, but it's all going down anyway. Pavo worked for thirty odd years, starting at *Michelin* first.

Last nine years he spent with his wife at the Family Court. The kids have grown up, not even visiting him, although he provided each with a flat, and now he builds this brick house on the top of a hill that will soon become a *shelter for students*. Thereafter, 59 year old Pavo will buy a round-the-world ticket, and go visit his old country.

Last night he listened to the news, the *Radio Belgrade*.

The light was off because of the bad reception, the volume was up because of Pavo's impaired hearing.

I had to lie down, exhausted after the whole day walking up and down the hill, calling about various jobs, explaining my weird C.V. I should write a book called *My Resume*. What *I haven't done,* or what I have made done in the last 40 years. *Dear Lord...*

The other day I went to check my free blood results, and it was *all good,* surprisingly, except for one little thing: thyroid gland. Well, Mandy had problems with it, maybe it's my share now, maybe I'll die at the same age her husband did, or the possums will have a go at me. Maybe I'll die before my father, hanging on a thread, that I feel guilty for not being around, although I did on and off for the last ten years, as well as the first twenty years of my life.

I'm grateful for *these* words coming at me, as if they were godsend, I'm grateful I can see the back of my soul, grateful I can share bread with a fellow man...

Last night Kiro cooked a dinner for us all, bought everything, no big invitation dramas:

I'll make you something finger licking good tonight, and it was.

I read the paper for him, the ads for a kitchen hand. There was one at the restaurant Beck 46, so I met him after work. Gino, the barbershop owner, never looked happy to see me, or his face was sour all the time.

We walked through the *Dee Why Arcade*, greeted the cleaner Jozo, who chatted with an old fat guy in front of a café that happened to belong to him.

He asked Kiro *where he was from*, frowning upon his answer, as though he'd bitten a rotten fish. He was Greek...

Kiro still addressed him nicely. To me he explained that Greeks hate Macedonians, because they conquered the part of ancient Macedonia, that they now call Greece, so they don't like having another *real* Macedonia next to it. Maybe it reminds them of who they really are...

Kiro said Macedonia used to spread all the way to *Thessalonica* and that people in that region could still speak Macedonian. But if they do then they have to pay a fine. A guy from there had to pay $500 because he called a donkey in Macedonian, so he escaped to Australia.

Why not to Macedonia?

Because it was poor, and meant to be divided between Serbia and Greece that already buys properties there, building factories, being the part of the European Union, *because they can.*

For some reason, the Balkans remained the haunted backwoods throughout the history that everybody claimed a piece of, as if it were a cake one wants to have and eat it too...

The whole day yesterday Kiro waited for me to drop by the *Gino's Barber Shop for Gents*. I forgot I said I'd stop by at lunchtime. I waited for the *Godot* bricklayers around here until 11 a.m. and then (after I did some writing), I rolled down the Kay Road.

I was still looking for work, reading *The Manly Daily* positions vacancies with all the experiences necessary, *RSA, MR, HR, OHS* a must, and, of course, none of it was in my Resume unless I lied about it.

It started puzzling me that after twenty years of trying (not so hard, apparently), I could never get a waiter job, although I already had one in my father's restaurant when I was 12. Then I didn't understand anything, picking up plates and silverware, bringing drinks to the inpatient guests forgotten by the thieving waiters.

One time Joško, the cook, had disappeared with all the money from the register. My father immediately jumped in his car and drove off. He pulled over to pick him up hitching. Blinded by the sun the poor guy didn't recognize my dad's car.

At random my father would shove them inside a tiny restroom and then go through their pockets, because *he told them a million times not to carry any cash on 'em while working!*

Their pockets emptied, their heads hanging down, they'd come out probably forgetting the most of the orders.

The guests would then shout at me to bring this and that.

At the end of the day I'd get 10,000 dinars, a red bill with *Tito on a horse* that I couldn't even spend on the ice cream and comic books. I could have started saving then, but everybody was too busy to let me know. Everything evolved around *bring this and that*. At the end of the day it still kept going. The spit-roasted lamb would be ready; my father carried it above his head turning it around as if slow dancing while all the German tourists pop their bulgy blue eyes out ordering.

Later on a couple of guitars would start strumming away softly and then my mother would shine letting her voice go, as if it were a little bird in someone's hands.

The nights ended at dawn, with plenty of beer to drink and meat to eat. The grill was on after 2 a.m. The beer machine as well. It's how I got drunk for the first time; nobody could see me pouring it.

Everybody was busy singing and drinking. After a few beers, my legs were numb, and I couldn't stand up as a couple of girls waved at me to come along to a disco.

Fudo, rest in peace, paddled a little dinghy (the one I used during the day) in the middle of the night, wearing a varicose vein sock with *JAWS* imprinted on it. It was colored red *to attract the sharks from the big oceans.*

Wrapped in a white sheet, singing and screaming drunk, he threw a bunch of the same bills with *Tito on a horse* into the pitch-black sea. They floated on it like red autumn leaves. A few guys jumped in to save them from drowning. One could still hear him singing and yelling.

Afterwards, when finally everybody went to sleep, I woke up with a strangest noise I never heard before. I wasn't alone in that big spare room. I could hear a woman's voice moaning and whispering mixed with Fudo's drunken muttering *Djurdjicaaa...* It was her name.

My father slept only a couple of hours nightly, going to bed last and getting up first to drive to Makarska and pick up the restaurant supplies.

One morning he hit the brakes driving too fast, and a whole body hit him from behind. It was drunken Rasim who fell asleep in the backseat overnight. My father kept driving and yelling at him. It didn't help the mother of all hangovers he suffered from.

Fudo would get up around noon wearing white, ironed pants, smiling and dealing with the books. The days rolled one into another sunny and bright. Many people came from Sarajevo and other places to visit and enjoy their vacation, eating at the restaurant and sleeping at the organized private accommodations. It looked as if my father and Fudo were getting rich, but they could barely make their ends meet.

As the fall approached, it was time to go back home into the winter and snow, crossing the *Ivan's Pass,* and every year was the same. The business paid off only what was invested. One night there was screaming and fighting, and someone grabbed a knife from the kitchen. It probably made the German tourists' day.

They could go home satisfied that we were still *savage people*—it would have been better *if they conquered us together with the Italians.* Every year they came back to remind us. They didn't have to pay much for it. It was way cheaper then waging wars, enjoying the best free things in the world.

Now as I read these ads for waiters here, and all the requirements for it, I'm sure no one shoves them into toilets to rummage through their pockets. It's democracy, free will and power-of-rights' world, when people probably steal more than ever.

Even though it's all computerized and organized, you can see it in their eyes. They're trained to steal politely, smiling at you. Just don't be savage. Smile and the world will smile back at you. It's one of the first things our English teacher taught us. No matter what you do, just smile, say *sorry & thanks,* and the world is yours.

If you talked about the truth, differences, mentalities, color of the skin, philosophies, religion, love, you were gone too far...

Still we applied for Kiro, since he wanted another job to be able to finally ship his container full of second hand stuff *(a kilo of shirts $3 only!)* to Macedonia. He wanted to work night shifts as a kitchen hand, no matter cutting people's hair the whole day.

And look at me, can't find a job, *what's my problem?*

I promised to myself half a dozen years ago that I'd never be a kitchen hand again. I can't even remember why I had made that promise, but at the back of my mind I still keep it. Maybe because they never let me be a waiter. Every time I remembered my father's restaurant, I'd just put the plates down and walk out...

Maybe because I can't stand the way they lie to each other, thinking it's well hidden and not obvious at all... Maybe because I've seen too much dirty water in the sinks up to my elbows, and all the chefs slowly going mad imprisoned under their big hats... Maybe because my father worked so hard getting zilch in the end... Maybe it was his fault and I'm paying for it now... Maybe my mission is to witness and write about it, even though no one wants to know because *everybody knows*... Maybe because that's the way it is...

But I have learned one thing. Going there, to Beck 46, to help Kiro get a job, because he can't read or write his broken English, I have found out that at the same place they had live music. Now, that's something I'd been doing for more than twenty years, and it felt like I could get a job too.

The lesson is: *truly helping others without expecting anything in return, you might find help for yourself around an unexpected corner...*

Probably I won't get it either, but I went there yesterday feeling like a person, offering something I was really skilled for, a unique experience I've built throughout the years of my roaming around the world, washing dishes, digging the dirt, painting tired old walls, scratching them with my nails, bringing them back into life so one could be surrounded by them—maybe it's something I'm not good at in the end: *being walled in.*

As I read all these *ad hoc* ads, I find out I can't even do most of it because they require own transportation.

Why don't I get a cheap car? I guess, no excuses there...

It's my funny situation where I have a car sitting in Portland, Oregon, and I'm in Dee Why, New South Wales. Throw the coin in the air, *mate* or *buddy.* They both stand for the same thing but sound as an empty fart. Every time I hear them my skin cringes.

G'day, mate & no worries, buddy, while the day is as good as it gets, and the worries are what you make of them. Who is your *mate,* really? I'll tell you—it's when I go with Kiro, and we face an obstacle, and the obstacle says *come tomorrow,* the boss is not around, and we leave the name and number, not hanging around for too long, (even though I was tempted to check out a local singer/songwriter). We went back home so that Kiro prepares our dinner. Because he wanted the three of us to try something delicious, and delicious it was...

Pavo, Kiro, and myself, a little Yugoslavia that doesn't exist *over there* anymore. But it does in Australia. A true mate-ship, sharing, being together. I ended up washing the dishes, and I only mention it as an inevitable fact that no matter how much you avoid something, it gets to you in the end. But in small doses it's fine.

So, the next day the deal was to go back to Beck 46, bring my

CD's and talk to Hanif, the manager, about Kiro as well.

A gorgeous day, blue skies, 27 degrees. Kiro left around 8 and I wrote till 11 waiting for the builders. They never showed up, and I headed down to Dee Why, checking the email, the usual stuff, calling about jobs, and this time going with my CD's, *offering something concrete.*

A ten minute walk down one of the Parades, Howard or Pacific, whatever. All the little apartment complexes, leafy streets, some people looking strange as if coming from a Monty Python show. But at the end the beach and the surf waited to top it all off like an endless masterpiece.

Asking for Hanif, he's busy. Stefan wants to know *what I'm after.* With a bald eagle eye look and the French accent, pouting his lips as if *my* English was broken. Funny how people climb up the ladder as soon as they feel a little bit of power, and then, by all means, politely or no, they want to know *what goes on…*

I need to talk to Hanif, and I'll wait…

He couldn't go past that because I live on the edge and it has become my life. For him to get a grip, he'd need to walk on the wild side a mile or two, but being a French *maitre d',* he couldn't avoid his Australian waitress wife speaking French with an English accent.

Boy, how life is funny sometimes, like a surrounding reality show…

And I'm waiting for Hanif, who must be Lebanese.

Since he is busy on line, I'm waiting with my CD's in a brown paper bag from Byron Bay. There I bought that sticker for my car with Rachel, and here I was now in Beck 46, waiting for Hanif, with that folded paper bag and a Byron Bay faded imprint on it.

If it all makes sense, then it must be above our limited minds. One can only admire it, or shrug shoulders, or whatever, but one has to follow it through, or just leave it behind and keep walking.

I asked if I could smoke a cigarette outside, while waiting.

Sho' (sure), no problem, *do you want something to drink?*

On a tight budget, I overheard that with domestic deafness (something I learned from Mandy and finally started using—*it worked!*). I got out, taking a seat at one of the tables.

The night before the whole place was screaming with lorikeets, now it was just sort of breezy cool, the lazy surf splashing the beach. A couple occupied the other table with menus and everything, and they had to pull it back to get some shade.

I felt a bit guilty sitting in the shade and just smoking, waiting for Hanif. The cigarette always gets me into some timing trouble. I stood up and crossed the street. I knew the waitress would be there any minute to ask me about drinks and food. It's good to just know certain things, it gives one time to maneuver, but one has to be extremely careful with the timing. One second and it's too late, or too early.

Behind my back, I could hear a couple taking my spot. The screeching noise of a moving table was muffled by a passing car. On the other side of the street I stumped the cigarette butt into the ground underneath a pine tree and sat on a public bench gazing at the rolling emerald.

It never ceased to amaze me how all those people didn't get it. They simply took it for granted. It fired me up to load them all up and ship back to China, India, England, Ireland, Italy, Yugoslavia …

Why couldn't they just enjoy this pristine environment?

Indeed, lots of kids and dogs were happily swimming, playing in the sand, some surfers were always riding those waves, the surf rescue was there looking bored, mean and ready. But other than that, the most of the people had their eyes glued to the horizon.

Maybe one shouldn't expect them to jump for joy, but I couldn't beat the feeling they were just unhappy not getting over themselves. I mean, I know life's hard, but just seeing that emerald cover of green and blue in its magic rolling motion—that soft golden sand under your feet, after an icy January in Portland, it's all one could wish for.

Maybe that's the thing: they haven't spent a cold and rainy January in Portland yet, but they will have a cold July here. Maybe they simply didn't want to think about it…

My writing is like a truncated email sometimes.

It should be done the way Cendrars or Celine did it. A gained momentum goes without stopping, otherwise there's too many breaks, various events, more or less important, as all of them put in one place cause a bottleneck effect, interrupting a continuous flow that like a river should carry it all to a common estuary…

Hanif eventually showed up, behind me, while I was going through my backpack determined to sit and wait, as if the time ceased to exist. Today it's already two days later, and whatever happened then becomes irrelevant now, since some other situations took part in it, pushing the previous ones behind. Taking it all apart might result in trivial little pictures that get no grip in creating something bigger, but what's big and what's small in life depends on both individual and universal rules.

Therefore Cendrar's *Gold* sounds fresh although it occurred two centuries ago. The way it's written is still alive, any time one picks up and opens the book at any page.

Hanif was refreshing, a person with a soul and tact. Maybe because of his managing position that put him above others, but in his dark eyes one could see respect—a bit of a curious caution too, since I sat there and waited with a mysterious message.

As I gave him the CD's and explained about Kiro, he was relieved but still professional and at least treated me as a dignified and equal human being. Even though he never called back.

Now that's the one—*is hope good or not?*

In my country one says *he, who hopes, dies hungry.*

Maybe, but he who hopes and, *surtout*, believes, proceeds with dignity toward the same ending. It's how one feels about oneself that really matters, the world has already gone mad.

After that I was gone—*to the beach!*

There were no reasons strong enough to beat the crisp living picture unfolding in front of my eyes. What if it rains tomorrow (it was predicted, but it never happened), or I die, or… Well, a few hours later Kiro almost cut me in two—*where were you all day?*

I forgot completely I was supposed to stop by the *Gino's Barbershop for Gents* during lunchtime. But I was on the beach, and after that I went to, again, try and sort out my Medicare card.

The Police was looking for you, Sheriff himself!

He was all scared and worried because early that morning they stopped him at *the gate*, asking if he knew *a man*, and they took his details too, so that all confused he forgot the name of the person they looked for.

It started with an M or N, I don't know!

Great, my last name starts with *M!* Once life spins you in a rinse cycle, if that makes you paranoid, you start imagining all kinds of possibilities, and those are numerous. Anything can happen, somebody can misunderstand this, believe that, say whatever, and all you got is your honesty to feed off…

Again, a few hectic days went by…

Looking for work and a place to live is actually one of the biggest and most adventurous jobs. You always walk on the edge, when a push of destiny comes to shove, in or out, left or right. It turned out that the police were looking for some Spanish guy Carlos for whatever reason that Pavo mentioned, and I forgot.

It all slowly became history, just another sunny day with a bit of a cool breeze. But the night before, Kiro and I were both scared, thinking of all the possibilities that might have followed our bad luck. Once the police come to your door, they use all their means to justify it. In the end, nobody likes to look like a fool, making mistakes and being laughed at. How many jokes about stupid policemen, don't you think once in a while they like to look and act smart?

And that could be someone's bad luck, or in the end just a waste of expensive time. Every move one makes today costs a couple of bucks. Therefore people stay at home, those who have one. The others look for it, and in the rats' race, *who is the cat?*

One makes big and shiny pictures on the passing buses like: *be the cat in the rat race* or *your skin should shine because you're worth it!*

One sits behind an actual desk inventing a witty little ditty, somebody that has a mortgage to pay, maybe a wife that is addicted to poker machines, or maybe a semi-retarded kid that needs an expensive treatment.

People like me, who don't have the Medicare card, have to make one happen, and in those cases either magic or shit happens. One doesn't need an action packed thriller full of shooting and wrecked cars.

The biggest nerve racking blockbuster could be one about an average rat standing in lines in front of various counters, while behind those, other rats sit encaged imposing the rules and regulations plus the echo of their ordinary madness they leave at home every morning and face every night.

It's a game of escaping into a temporary oblivion. It's a pure gambling and the luck of the draw applies in most of the cases. Even if you have all the paperwork required, you risk stepping on someone's toes simply because they were *mal baisé* (sexually frustrated), excuse my French. Or because *you* were *mal baisé,* or not at all.

That opens another dimension, one could also mention Michelangelo and his life as an example. But since most of the rats have never heard of him, or they remember only the convenient parts, then—*what's the point?*

If I mentioned that Michelangelo believed in *less sex, longer life* philosophy, who'd want *that* and any philosophy altogether?

Eventually, life brings us to those long lines when we need help, like any overheated engine, and then any performance is out of question. Instead of *mal baisé,* one is then just *mal dans sa peau.*

But I was exalted that day. I went to the little Dee Why family practice packed with different bugs, flu, little brats rubbing their eyes because their mothers let them lick the carpet in the waiting room or let them roll on supermarket floors, while they were busy investigating some skin products, because *they're worth it…*

Still, the day was bright and sunny outside, and after all I had on my plate for the last 40 years, it was quiet amazing and soothing. It was more than sufficient. It was maybe all I had in the end, all I was looking for. Plus, the coincidence that the receptionist spoke my native language made it all seem like a genuine little fairy tale.

You reach the end of the world, a nice little corner, you go to see a doctor because you can, because you couldn't for five years, because when you had to, you ended up paying some astronomical figures, and that made you shun medicine altogether.

Suddenly, you feel like you're free, and you think to yourself *this is real democracy,* no matter screaming brats and skin products, poker machines, and so on. At least you can stroll down to a doctor's office, say *g'day,* chat a little about the weather, say *A,* sign the paper, get out in the sunshine, and get your vitamin D…

The receptionist appeared to be very friendly, concerned in a lighthearted way. I gave her my Medicare number on a piece of paper I was given years ago. Before my card was supposed to be issued. Then Mandy and I separated and I never got the card. I had that piece of paper valid till 2008, have never even used it, but I kept it with all the million other little papers and things pilling up as I circumnavigated around my life.

When a few months ago I had another kidney stone attack, I thought to myself: why wouldn't I just give them my little Australian Medicare number?

Mind you, I was giving birth to a 3 mm stone then, but I still remembered my last $1600 bill from a previous, even smaller stone, when they hooked me up to morphine till my fingernails went blue. I couldn't sit or lie down, I couldn't breathe, but *Sister Morphine* took care of it, almost taking my breath away...

So, the admin woman, as she took my details to strip my skin off later, happened to have a daughter living in Melbourne. We were in the *St. Vincent's Hospital,* Portland, where they sometimes write off the bills as charity *(if one can't pay),* but I still didn't get *why I had to pay the first time* since it was the same *Providence* branch... They still had me on their computer...

Anyways, for some reason, my magic *Australian Medicare* number worked, the stone also got pissed out after a whole tormenting week, and now, in Dee Why, I was just going to have a little check up and, also, do the Infertility test...

Even though I already did one in Vancouver, WA, jerking off in the hospital's little pantry (no fancy magazines with naked women— just me surrounded by tired brooms and other cleaning utensils), Rachel thought why not do another one here, since it was free...

She was born frugal.

Let me digress here a bit...

I have changed a fair amount in the last few years. Before I used to stand up for my believes more, being extremely proud and argumentative. I thought people were blind leading the blind. Maybe they still do, maybe they know it or don't. *Whatever.*

Life has brought me to the point where I started having crucial pains. Crucified inside I was bleeding from those nine-inch nails produced by tormented consciousness, and I was literally dying inside.

My soul was dying.

Whether I wanted it or not, I had to change. Like that old fortunetelling lady in Brisbane told me, after I painted her little business room behind the veggie restaurant (that belonged to the same family), she said:

In life there are changes and all you can do is accept them. The more you oppose, the more painful it will be. You still have some lessons to learn, but you're on the right path.

Something like that, since I never remember exactly the dialogues from the past. I never have that *Dictaphone* when needed, as most of the time it wouldn't be appropriate, so I have to rely on my memory shaken by my opposing and coping with it, instead of just accepting. But, hey, let's admit it's not easy, and most of the time we just don't know.

We can only follow our inner voices, and even that would be a blessing. Because one mainly follows the writings on the buses nowadays. Writings on the walls are outdated and overrated unless they come from the same advertising source.

You know what I mean anyway, and if you don't—*isn't that the point?*

You're either opposing to changes yourself or you simply just go with the flow, but *what flow?*

The flow I went with was still the same old river that carries me spirally back to my heart, and I know it because I feel it.

That should be enough for me. It's where I stopped a few years ago, or maybe even a few months ago. I stopped being concerned whether other people do the same, whether they know or don't, or whatever their reasons are. It was hard and hurting just to see one straying and not being able to help because one, for whatever reason, went with his own flow.

It appears to be the same one we all follow, like when we hop on a long bus ride to Sydney and then everybody gets off in the same hive, because all roads lead to Rome, but *with what purpose?*

Victims of comfort or desire, or even love, like in a song I wrote years ago. But one cannot be the victim of love. It's just the title. One is the victim of a no-win game one plays and calls love. What's the name of the game—*that's the question.* Love is not a game, as well as health or hunger. But one can play with it, one can gamble, if that's all one knows and follows.

The *RSL* club is full of poker machines and hard working people feeding them. On the TV, and some buses, one warns about it, but in the *RSL* clubs, read: high-end mini casinos, one puts up with it. There is a strong security built around it, all big smiles and membership fees, free soda and coffee, just push the button…

Pavo received the letter last night calling him to appear in front of the *Board Directors of the Club* because of the incident that occurred.

What incident, get fucked, yells hardworking Pavo, a bit tipsy, *I'll show them the incident; they just want my money!*

I happened to be with him that night, because I helped him totter there after a few wines he had. The Tongan security guy politely wouldn't let him in, as he was drunk, and since a drunk never agrees with that, the security had to call the manager, who wasn't really in the best mood that night, grumpy and not polite at all. He just said to Pavo to get lost, and then Pavo replied with *fuck off!* It happened that the manager spoke the same *effing* language, saying *fuck you,* and off we went.

Have I done anything to anybody, have I disturbed anybody, have I caused any damage?

Pavo goes on, pouring another plum brandy…

And if they want to control people drinking, why don't they control them gambling? Why don't they put limitations on how far could people gamble and just say enough spending money for tonight, you gambled your daily bread away!

I have to agree with Pavo. Not that he should go there drunk or drink at all, but if drinking is a sin, why gambling isn't, why there are no speeding limits imposed?

Many people gambled their houses, jobs, marriages, and lives away—why isn't there a, let's say, $100 limit? But then the whole deal goes down the tubes, the whole crazy world falls apart, all the machines, barkeeps, waiters, and all the *Tongan-Maori-Samoan* security muscles go to work where?

A factory?

Well, some people are always there, even while we're sleeping. The perpetuity goes on. More machines, poker or other, more food, more medication, more iron sheets…

On the TV last night they showed a documentary about the cleaning force of Australia. *All the broken-English immigrants cleaning our offices before & after business hours,* said the presenter, and then an old woman spoke up, half her teeth missing, saying that *she had no time to drink a glass of water from all the hard work…*

It was a golden country twenty years ago, sighs Pavo, interrupting, *it's all BS now, mate!*

They build a quasi-communism, that's what they do, and look what happened in our country—it shouldn't have happened, to let brotherly people kill each other!

We all lived in peace respecting each other's customs and religions…here, as a requirement, they let you in as a doctor or engineer, but then they send you off to work in a factory!

Before that, on the TV, a charming gray haired Australian painter was doing a portrait of the Queen, and he was so fulfilled about it, probably accomplishing his lifelong dream. A happy chap talking to his Queen Mother and even portraying her, allowing himself a few innocent jokes to what she tactically replied as any mother, never changing the posture, never allowing the lines of her face to show anything different than one did on the former successful portraits displayed in the portrait room.

There were even a few contemporary ones!

Only her face was successfully getting older, and then she just smiled and disappeared behind the door into another room heavy with gold and laces, leaving the happy painter chap like a kid at play.

He went on explaining to us mortals about the job he did, line by line. His ultimate wish was to present the Queen as realistic as possible, not too much shadow on the right, not too much light on the left. Not too many details around. Just the Queen and her blessed disposition.

What a difference to the documentary they showed about Michelangelo the other night. Two painters, centuries apart, two lives, two worlds, two visions, two believes… The maestro was destroying the most perfect drawings, *because art must appear to be created effortlessly.*

Toward the end of his life he questioned the role of an artist and art itself mainly fearing God and His Judgment, while our happy Aussie chap made sure the very same Queen's smile is reproduced and preserved time and time again…

————

At the doctor's, life was unbearably cozy. It's about how people treat you. Mister Gajanan is one of the kindest persons I ever met. The way he greets you, shows you way in, a chair to sit, his voice full of respect, firmness and softness at the same time, with a big patient and peaceful smile that, by the way, resembled one of a cartoon-like baboon. It was confusing because he was nicer and gentler than any human I ever met.

After showing him my little kidney stone I carried across the Pacific, we arranged next appointment when I was to draw blood so he could proceed with all the tests. I was supposed to fast for twelve hours before 9 a.m. Saturday. The receptionist Mira was also nice, and we even spoke our own language, maybe a bit too much because she had offered to help me with my English before I had entered the room.

She maybe thought I spoke our language because I couldn't speak English, and I only did it to make it easier for her, because of *her* broken English. Also out of a sheer amazement that I could do it as if I was in a medical center back in Sarajevo.

Not that I would see any people from Tonga, Greece or India there, but it made the whole thing more amazing. For a moment it felt as if *that was it.* All the nations living together happily under the same sun…until I reached the *W* Mall.

Nothing wrong with the mall, it was almost like the Lloyd Center in Portland, minus the ice-skating field, plus the little cafés where people smoked on the terraces.

I was busy looking for *Medicare* and had to ask a few times for directions. As I finally found it, there was a long line inside and ten magic counters with ten women seated behind.

Numbers flicked on the screen and the little arrows pointed me to 5. This was not Mira from Doboj, this was a lady who made sure her smile was not too obvious and her skills are far advanced a few minutes ahead of any possible issue. No issues. *Just after the lunch break questions,* and anything that doesn't match them is thoroughly investigated.

No matter that Mira had already talked to someone on the phone, arranging everything for me just to pick my card up. This lady— strangely, I don't remember her name—made sure to politely and a bit dry let me know I'd have to prove my address and my living situation altogether.

She somehow even made me utter that I wasn't in the country for the last 3 years. I don't know how she did it. There was a certain imperial way about the whole polite and dry interrogation making one feel as if it was a *Missing Link* show, and then one gets nervous because something is always missing: a home, job, car, wife, child, pet...

They want to make sure that you genuinely are to reside and for that you are to show the proof that you lease your apartment for which you'd have to have paid 6 rents minimum and provide the proof that you have a steady income, or you could show the proof of an employment for which normally you got to have a place to live...

Or, if you lived overseas, to have the same proves that you did the same thing there...

If, like me, you are an immigrant with less than 2 years time required to have spent in Australia, for which again you'd need somehow to survive on your wits or savings, and they would, of course, graciously provide you with the Medicare card. But there I was in front of my counter number five not having any of it.

With Mandy I had it all because of the universal *women & children first* law. Once you leave the nest, you're pretty much on your own.

Thank God and Mandy, I had my Medicare provisional number on a stamped piece of paper valid till 2008, and it was still in the computer. The Counter Goddess made sure she did her job promptly and orderly, even though at home she probably didn't, but since she had to do it somewhere, my *M* card was declared lost, and I had to bring the proof of my address.

She gave me the form for my landlord to fill out. He was to describe where he knew me from and if my intentions were good. Now that would be a mission impossible because Pavo hardly reads and writes English at all. But was I a complete idiot to tell them that too and make my life a nerve racking nightmare?

In numerology, since I got number 5 in my year of birth, it says that those people sometime persist for their own bad. Funny, I had the counter number 5 too. The old lady who did my prenatal horoscope in Brisbane also said that number 5 means learning and starting all over again, so I did.

I lined up and this time got the number 2. She was not imperial at all and pretty human at that. But either something was already marked in the computer, or I was simply doomed. She basically repeated the same deal.

OK, no problem, I'll do it your way, I'll take this form to Pavo and we'll fill it out together…

As the Bosnian Imam in Portland said:

God loves you so much that, even when he is to punish you for your sins, instead of throwing a boulder on you, He first crumbles it in tiny little pebbles and then it's how you get it, piece by piece…

Pavo, no doubt, is a good and hard-working man, but only a human dealing with his own boulder, actually building it in front of his existing house. He builds another one, pulling this one apart, rebuilding it, and putting *all the pebbles* into a mighty *brick house*.

Therefore he landscapes for another landlord. There is always a Lord's Lord till the Almighty Lord Godot comes along, never showing up...

Work hard, pay your bills, taxes, and your club membership. Be a good *Dago*, otherwise you may as well go back where you came from.

Love it or leave it!

To cope with it most people drink and gamble, which makes it difficult for finding sober moments and filling out forms. What's more, it took Pavo days to find his Medicare card, because his Medicare number had to be on the form as well, and the signatures...

Now that was confusing even for the counter ladies: signature of a person making the declaration. Declared at...on the...day of...20... And then it needs another signature of person before whom Declaration is made, without mentioning who would that be.

Maybe it's because I have recently arrived from the *Republican United States* that I simply couldn't fully grasp the *Royal Ways*. So, a few days later, I went to the bank and got a statement showing my address. The clerk there actually explained to me how it worked, but now I still can't remember, and that day I went to the W Mall again anyway.

I also brought my *ABN* number with me, and on my way there, before getting on a bus, one old lady in front of me moved very slowly ahead with her little shopping cart. It looked as if she wasn't going to make it neither in nor outside of the bus. She got stuck on the first step and everybody waited for a miracle.

I grabbed her cart behind her and lifted it up while she purchased her ticket. It didn't look that hard, but nobody did anything about it, and one would have waited forever.

She smiled at me gratefully and I thought maybe it was the sign I was going to make it this time!

Help and you'll be helped!

The main thing is you do it spontaneously, from your heart.

The *W* Mall makes one feel like back in the States, and it's even better. People look free, more relaxed, maybe a bit too much, without seeming bothered by it. The gaudy items are all on display, one only needs money to pay for it, most of them work for it, and in democracy, a royal one at that, nobody stops you spending it. *Au contraire!*

It's where the mass production and consummation laws set in.

Paris Hilton and the likes have introduced the guide lines for young girls, and, *no worries,* there are seeming counterparts like *Avril Levigne* and the likes to complete the variety. How many girls wear *The Ramones* T-shirts, and they still look like pin ups changing the style a bit, from glamour to punk, until they combine it in the end, and no one even notices the difference.

It's all good! They're only kids exposing their hips and kidneys and, of course, they don't sleep around, *they're good kids.* The bad ones are always those that the writers of history classify as losers for whatever applicable reason.

But I was *only* 41, and still on my mission, through the trappings of a new world, to get my little Medicare card. This time I got number 10. *5 + 5, there you go!* I even got a chair to sit on. The counter lady number 10 was a double dry martini, not so much imperial. More like an Australian *Desperate Housewife* version on a high horse of womanhood galloping through the desolate world of trivial mankind.

Every time it amazes me more and more. Aussie guys think they rule with their rugby attitude of men who don't surrender, but women here are mainly interested in TV shows and the attitude of starlets and, as always, they never stopped being interested in guys who stick to their self-esteem, which again might lead to a rugby attitude. But there's a fine line to walk and become, say, a genuine lawyer-surfer-barkeep, or simply be a spunky hunk out of a latest fashion magazine.

At times, it's only *Aussie, Aussie, Aussie! Oi, Oi, Oi!…*

I have also heard that women here are attracted to Europeans because of their culture and *je ne sais quoi*. But it is not that obvious, at least I haven't witnessed many cases. Maybe South Americans have more luck with their Latin charm, or simply because Aussies like to travel there—many like to travel anywhere, just buy a ticket and off they'll go!

As I look out the panoramic window, the clouds are rolling in dark and heavy. The sun breaks through occasionally, while the palms are dancing like willows in the wind. The autumn is slowly moving in. The summer is half way across the Equator.

The Medicare card hasn't arrived. It's already been a couple of weeks and it seems it didn't really matter I was at the counter number ten. The double dry lady had simply announced my card lost, gave me another form to fill out without even asking the proof of address. Because this time I didn't mention being overseas for three years since nobody asked.

She gave me another provisional number saying that my Medicare is valid till 2012, and that I'll receive my card in the mail, swiftly tearing my old one up. I should have kept it because my joy didn't last very long. After I thought I managed through the ordeal, excited I didn't have a good look at the new number.

It said: *this advice form valid only until 18/05/06.* My old number was at least valid till 2008. Tonight I guess Pavo and I will still have to go through the signing procedure of the declaration and tomorrow I'll go to the W Mall hopefully being third time lucky...

Here, one gets up between 5.30 and 6 a.m.

Usually Stipe slides the old Japanese door and pulls Pavo's leg. It's his favorite part of the day, realizing that Pavo is fast asleep, that Pavo is just Pavo, and that he'll never change.

Pavo builds and destroys. He drinks, gambles, and yells half deaf, repeating the same old mistakes, working hard every day.

Stipe is the seeming opposite, always on time, not talking much, also working hard, but putting everything back in its place, his clothes neatly folded, his room in order—*he even has a private bathroom.*

He goes to the club regularly, having a dinner and a beer, but he never gambles, looking like bald Clint Eastwood's when he smiles, keeping out of trouble ever hanging around like a totem pole.

Pavo and Stipe, like east and west, an Orthodox and a Catholic conceived and born in the same corridor frequented by most ancient armies that left mixed blood traces of different cultures behind.

Pavo and Stipe, speaking the different dialects of the same language, Montenegro and Dalmatia, at the first sight as if they had nothing in common. But both were arid and proud, washed by the same sea that one day took them away to the other side of the world, where they work together and sleep with only a gyp rock wall with an unearthly Japanese drawing between them.

While the war raged in their native Yugoslavia, they worked *for the man* in Australia, landscaping, maintaining his property, and somehow he's from Yugoslavia too… Every half a century a war was waged, a habit inherited from all those different armies passing through.

As the Russian Revolution skipped Capitalism and jumped from Feudalism right into Socialism, Yugoslavia followed their example, and then again was attacked by Germans. After a tanker of blood spilled, getting the monkey off their back, *70%* of people were illiterate, swamping the cities, leaving the fields and plows to their old fathers.

The Revolution didn't eat its kids. They wanted to play, building castles in the sand. Maybe because originally they were kids at heart…

But it's the name of the game that matters. Freedom is not a game, and many use it to get what they want, or what they think they want.

What a child knows in the end?

What supermarket you take him to, what TV channel he's brainwashed with, what food chain he's hooked up on? And then one calls it Freedom...

If a human is a child at heart, a wise old toothless man is nothing but a child returning to the source. It's the name of the game that matters. And those who know it standing behind the curtain with crooked smiles, they are the ones to blame.

They want to play a little too, the only way they learned, the only way they know. Shall we send them to the corner and make them even more stubborn and mad?

Maybe there's a better way, but who'll introduce it, how many prophets one needs, how many scientists, how many philosophers?

Is Love God, Heart or Serotonin? Come on, make up your minds, it's time to flip the coin once for all, or you'd rather just flip it for the sake of the game! *Head or tails?*

It's probably all connected, as usual, and one is just to find the right balance. The presence of one side can only be grasped against the potential absence or background of the other.

―――――――

My writing is clandestine at times.

Yesterday morning I was going to get up chased by a huge tidal wave of thoughts and ideas ready to hit the shore. But Pavo was home this weekend, although he was still asleep snoring.

I thought about sneaking out with my laptop. He could have woken up anytime and seen me writing.

The psychologists and writers are the biggest fools, he said once bitterly.

I even agreed with him up to a point.

I'm sure that all my not finding work by him would be *because of writing.* Since I have to worry about the roof over my head, I'd rather do it when nobody's around. It even sounds better then, one can only hear the birds and the breakers in the distance.

Out of all yesterday's thoughts, I do remember one clearly.

It's about my Medicare card again. I was there for the third time already a few days ago now, counter number 9, and I even remember her name. Whatever one does three times, it starts to feel familiar. One develops some kind of a routine, being able to pay more attention to details.

Theresa had Mediterranean features, dark hair, dark eyes, *Greek profile,* and that human attitude, a human touch, if you wish. She was there to soothe people's worries not shooting them down in flames, and then using an extinguisher from a safe distance.

She said it would take 2 to 3 weeks before I receive my card in the mail. Because it comes from Canberra, and they have to check it all up, *love.*

It felt good just to hear that word. *Love.* People should use it more. Some of them do, especially when they sell or want you to sign something.

Yesterday morning I lay in bed and felt like crying as my thoughts were taking off. Not only I couldn't write them down, but shortly afterwards we got up, and boiled some eggs in a big sauce pan, *because I couldn't find a smaller one.*

Pavo added a couple more with little sausages to use up the boiling water. For some reason one of his eggs broke, probably because they were cold straight from the fridge, and I gave him one of mine.

This morning I took the lid off, the saucepan was still there with the same used water, only the eggs were all gone, he took them to work.

After we had our little breakfast, off we went to start digging the sewer trench around the house. Goodbye enlightening thoughts, now there were others coming, some of them enlightened by heavy lifting, but most of them becoming burdensome as one starts working for the man.

The man, no matter how good or bad he is, wants things done *his way.* Rare are those who consult others and follow the saying that *two heads know better than one.* They mainly follow the principle that *no head knows anything.* And, finally, because I keep digressing, that one thought that I still remember…somehow, unintentionally, fits well just here.

The thought is very conventional, said and heard about trillion times by now, and periodically still repeated, time after time:

What am I fucking doing to myself?

It was, at first, related to the Medicare card, but it can pretty much be related to anything one does, because he who does, he does it to himself first, whatever it is…

My address, my Medicare card, digging the trench, walking around Sydney and getting blisters on my tiptoes… It's all my own doing, if not my own making, so why do I keep going at it? It's not Medicare's fault I left three years ago, and came back three years later. Where have I been?

What was I doing? *Why?*

And then one digs harder and harder, breaking the sandstone and limestone, pushing the wheelbarrow along the trench and then crossing a wobbly little bridge made of used plywood to unload it on the old driveway and cover the holes in the ground for a new and better one *with electronic gates…*

There is a reason why, from the very beginning. The way I was brought up, the things I was taught and believed in, what I've become, the mistakes I've made out of my dreams still pushing the envelope.

And then you look around, this view, it will be pulled apart in a month or two, but it's still the same old view bathing in the sunshine caressed by the breeze while the ocean glitters like gold melting on the horizon.

I'm to leave it in a few days, and probably, *likely,* come back, when the view is gone, when one builds another one, better or worse, when *this and that* happens.

Why don't I stay then? Or why don't I stay there, with Rachel, my old father, mother, sister, little Michael...

I have completely forgotten to write about my Infertility test...

I did it once in Vancouver, SW Washington Clinic, last year, and I did it twice because the first time they made a mistake, didn't pick the specimen or something—never mind my having to jerk off in a laundry room so turned on with brooms and stuff and the whole infertility thing... I remembered the times when I was careful about not making babies, and there I was, of a sudden, finding out if I could.

Rachel wanted to investigate all the imaginable possibilities why she couldn't get pregnant... In Switzerland she finally did, but it turned out to be a miscarriage, and everything became thousand times worse. I also started to question everything with the same old *what I am doing to myself* doubt. Although I had to jerk off in the SW Washington hospital pantry room twice, it still was a high-tech experience in comparison to my infertility test here in Sydney. Here it goes...

Everything started with Dr. G.'s kind disposition. Everything seemed feasible and life was just another beautiful day outside the little family practice. It's not Dr. G.'s fault that it isn't. If everybody followed his example even 10%, this world would still be a better place.

He kindly sent me across the street to the *Kingsway Medical Centre,* from where I was to go to the *Henry Moir Pathology Lab* and get all the instructions. Even there the nurse was humanly oriented, just as her job needed her to be. She gave me two little containers—*as if she knew I was going to have to do it twice (again)!*—with all the necessary instructions and lots of cotton to use for wrapping the container and keep it warm on my way to the lab.

Keep it in the sun, if you can, on your way here!

The couriers leave at 9, 11 and 2 p.m. As I have just missed the 2 p.m. one, plus I'd have to go home and bring it back, I still didn't get how was the specimen going to be examined within 1 hour of collection. But, the nurse encouraged me with her genuine smile and kind disposition, and off I went. I was to do it the first thing Monday morning.

Of course I wasn't going to tell anybody. They would find the whole thing just a stupid waste of time, plus, they all sound like professional love makers with broken marriages and a couple of kids behind, and infertility to them would probably sound not manly enough. Well, I have never thought about it as a possibility in my case either. I began to believe I was maybe cursed by Mandy, or her kids, or God Himself…

The test I did in Vancouver said that Motility of my sperm was a bit bellow normal, *but it was still 80% okay.*

Once for all I was to make sure, here in Australia, *for free,* since I had Medicare.

Monday morning I waited for everybody to leave, put all the curtains on, and then waited till 8 a.m. I thought to myself, if I have to be there before 9, and if it has to be delivered within 1 hour, I should at least try and do it between 8 and 8.30…

And what about the other patients, what if there's a long line ahead of me and the courier leaves without my warm little specimen?

Somehow I did it, not really turned on at all. The whole thing started to look like an official jerking off, while other people had normal sex, although some like it hot and kinky…

The waiting room was full of sick & injured pretty much looking *normal,* but maybe not having sex at all, and so they became a little unhappy and weary. They probably stopped masturbating a long time ago and continued stroking their minds, which in 8 out of 10 cases, ends up an inevitable casualty.

Two British-Skittish climaxed receptionists were pretty alarmed when I showed them the specimen. If I brought blood or urine, or a piece of shit in that little container, it'd all look more like the usual stuff they deal with. What's more:

Who told me to bring it here, and the courier won't even be there before 11!

I just couldn't believe it...

Therefore some people avoid going to the doctors. Some people just live happy. They respect the universal laws and try not to upset God. They try to be grateful and humble. Not arrogant, and not stuck-up. But if one comes from an imperial heritage, acting so for hundreds of years, it's hard just to switch to republican, which didn't seem to be the best solution either.

After she made a couple of phone calls, it turned out I was misinformed. *That human nurse* had happened to be on call and not directing me properly...

All that was happening in the Fisher Road, since it was closer to home and had a better specimen delivery timing. I have actually made a mistake finding the place and first went to the Beaches radiology, where they had a lab with a really nice receptionist, who, unfortunately couldn't help me because I was ordered to a different lab.

I was still determined to go where it all started, warming the little container in my hands as if it were a frozen little bird. I wasn't just going to throw it away after all, and *how many times was I to jerk off anyway?*

If someone gave me a hand, maybe it'd have been fun, but it began to feel more and more like a lost case screwball comedy. Maybe people won't even like to read about it...

But what am I to do with the story, just push it somewhere at the back of my mind and pretend it never happened? And become just another casualty of Peace & Royal Democracy? Republican, or whatever...

I might make mistakes in life and maybe I'm a slow learner, but I'm a determined person, for my own good or bad. I'll push till they stop making a fool of myself in a way that suits them, even though *I* might have been making a fool of myself all along. I did it so many times that by now I have become an expert.

They always respect experts of some sort. They confuse it with a strong character not being quiet sure *what it feels and looks like.*

Another amazing fact was how many times was I to describe my case in front of a packed waiting room, all ears, idle and thirsty for gossip, while those old glass assed receptionists pierced me with their blue eyes, flashing their horse teeth at me?

And, I also had to pay for it. *It won't be more than $50 for sure!* She knew *that,* and she knew how to still tell me off while apologizing for their misinforming me at the same time. That was the receptionist at the *Kingsway MC,* and they obviously had already phoned her, because she finally knew it was the nurse on call that gave me the wrong information, but still:

We don't do this here, you wouldn't be able to leave it here anyway, you would have to go directly to the main lab!

And as she found out that I don't have a car to deliver the specimen in time:

Ah, that is strictly your problem, you're the one requesting the whole thing!

In other words, if you want your *bloody* sperm analyzed, then you make sure you buy a car, or catch a cab…

Why can't I just do it here?

She looked at me as if I uttered the most blasphemous curse, her eyes popping out.

Oh, no, you can't do it here!

It was like: *this is not a brothel, take your stupid business home!*

After the show, she still decided to put a heat pack on it and send it with the courier without charging me if it wasn't going to be successful. So that I could do it one more time and take it there myself.

My little infertility test turned out to be adventurous. The results were bad. There was almost a 4-hour gap between collection and examination. Dr. G. wanted me to do it again. And if it weren't good, he'd send me to see a specialist. The whole thing started growing like a beanstalk.

So now I had to wait 4 days before ejaculating again, and Dr. G. looked funny making sure I got it right—*no sex, no masturbation, no ejaculating*—as if it were a complicated disease. And it was because he didn't understand my question about 3 or 4 days. He thought I didn't understand the whole thing. The language barrier can be funny but can also become a nightmare full of explanations and forms of politeness that cause traffic jam…

I just nodded, no sex, no masturbation, no worries…

Let those stupid drunks do it, and all those healthy surfers and rugby players, and their *Paris Hilton* little copycats with *Dior* sunglasses on. I'll make sure I go to hospitals and jerk off in pantry rooms. A 4-day wait might make it all feel more exciting…

At home, Pavo and Paul yell at each other.

Half-deaf Pavo doesn't even hear the Paul's *f-offs,* but he did see the heating lamp on and goes berserk. Then he comes up here and yells more in our language.

Paul probably thinks he tells me things about him, and I, by the way, have no choice but to listen to it—listen to anything if I want to keep sharing Pavo's room. And Pavo tells, he tells stories from the past, full of wisdom and experience that nobody has time for…

Pavo's father was, before all, an honest man, who loved his neighbors first. He warned in an ancient dialect that *a bullet from his old gun would rip the lungs open* of whoever touched his Muslim neighbors.

My mother's family was once saved by their Serbian neighbors. They hid them from the Chetniks during the World War II.

Pavo grew up within the same tradition and kept respecting it.

Why kill innocent people, whatfo', it's bullshit, mate!

But killing is over, again, there's a break, *time out,* people run around fretting about money, they have no time to listen about the history.

Therefore the history repeats.

Pavo learned to work hard. He grew up in the country, on his father's big piece of land where it needed lots of work, and his father made sure everything functioned properly and orderly within a sacred tradition. Wherever he went, Pavo carried that legacy along with him...

In Sarajevo he was building the Butmir airport and the bridge in front of Skenderija. In Australia he worked long hours in factories, and even at present he works almost seven days a week.

He's 57, but he won't stop, therefore he keeps building here:

I build myself a monument!

Pavo builds while many just sit around shrugging shoulders fingers crossed. When he argued with Paul, it's not only because the heating lamp was on after midnight. Paul doesn't work, lives on welfare, occasionally gets drunk, and at times makes a fool of himself in the street. Pavo doesn't like Irish, Scottish, or English much. It's all the same to him. He thinks they have no culture, manners, cleanliness...

But in Australia he is to abide the English laws. He thinks they have been cooking and serving the ongoing meal of history and that no one will escape without paying them. His grandpa had told him once that *British boot is worse than German.*

Paul probably thinks that Pavo badmouths him, and he probably thinks I do the same because he can only hear *our bloody language* he can't understand. Maybe there's a bit of fairness in it, because many of our people came here not understanding a word of English still building most of the country...

I never said a word against Paul. I've just listened to Pavo, as we talked about other things. Nevertheless, Paul assumed a childish attitude testing me, as though I was here to squeeze him out. I wouldn't have lived in his stinky little mess of a room even if one paid me! But he made his own private hell thinking the world of it and being paranoid that someone would take it away. His own actions did it...

One morning I greeted him after talking to Pavo and I still was tuned into one of our old Yugoslavian songs, so when I saw Paul in the kitchen I have just uttered *eh-eh-hey,* which any of our people would understand, but Paul was being sarcastic about it:

It sounds like a donkey braying!

It was an early morning punch and I just rolled with it, but it was again a slap in my face, the same old lesson, *never be too friendly.* For that one has to control oneself most of the time being on alert, and since I like to be relaxed as much as possible, every once in a while I slip, forgetting not everybody is your friend, and also forgetting about all the little nuances in different languages, cultures and non-cultures.

I kept it to myself. Pavo just waited for any excuse to kick him out. Paul probably thought I was complaining to him anyway and started showing his teeth. My *love thy neighbor* attitude only made things worse. Avoiding conflicts made me look an easy prey.

Just slap him if he bugs you, advised Pavo, as he'd done it before.

I keep him only because my sister felt sorry for him, otherwise he'd be out long time ago, fucking bullshit!

Thursday night I went down to see Kiro, again getting *in trouble.*

Paul was drunk and all hyper, pumping the volume up, some inarticulate punk band that he used to be a bus driver for back in Ireland.

He yelled over the noise explaining it to Kiro with his Irish accent, while Kiro had trouble understanding the Australian one. I started translating for Kiro, automatically being helpful, a trait I developed since doing all the work for the Bosnian refugees in France, translating for the ex-prisoners of death camps, and later on for my parents…

Paul gave us the finger wave, slamming the door in our face.

Kiro looked at me puzzled: *shall I slap him around a bit?*

We were both surprised by his sudden reactions of a lunatic.

Well, Pavo was going to be home shortly, probably drunk too. It seemed unlikely they were going to have fun.

Kiro and I went to his room to watch a DVD, the room I originally came to check out, responding to Pavo's ad.

When I had first seen it my stomach turned around. It looked like *enough rope*. But Kiro re-arranged it, put a TV in, a fridge, little table, and plenty of other abandoned stuff that he collects from the streets.

The other night we went to Beck 46 to inspect our status and finally listen to some live music. Two girls were there sitting at one of the high tables, making it look like it had 5 long bare legs, while upstairs Hanif was polishing the cutlery.

The music had a break—we were either too early, or too late—so our quick choice was to talk to Hanif and see if we got the job. He said to give him more time to listen to the CD's and that they need a good kitchen hand, someone to *clean all the mess*, not *a pizza chef,* as Kiro had put in his Resume.

On our way down the music was wrapping up, and again we hesitated to join the girls. Looking back, they were wrapping their legs up too, leaving the table to stand on its one and only. They seemed to be happy with each other anyway, releasing some inarticulate screams that most of the tipsy girls do here *free & easy.*

They all seem to belong to the *Girls Rule* or *Girls Kick Ass* associations until they give birth to a child, or they hit 35 and start looking their real selves. Then they are frustrated and mean unless they're genuinely good persons, but that's universal.

They dusted off their brooms leaving in a brand new burgundy vehicle, as Kiro and I went back walking the same way so that he can pick up that thing he'd found, some sort of a big rack for clothes.

Somebody threw it out and it was brand new!

Kiro was entangled in his own version of hell. Ultimately, he wanted to ship a couple of containers more and never come back again.

It seemed that *each day had not enough trouble of its own,* as three drunken guys headed toward us clinking their bottles and releasing different sorts of inarticulate screams that supposedly meant *free & easy* as well.

They just couldn't pass us by without using their rugby intelligence, which seemed even funnier the more drinks they had. The alcohol had spread their wings, and they thought they looked mean enough to be stupid.

Why didn't they just use their famous *how are you going, mate?*

Instead, they uttered something like *you want some turkey, Turkish boys?*

He meant *Wild Turkey* bourbon, without realizing how lucky he was that Kiro didn't understand him. I wasn't going to translate and end up not only jobless, but in a drunken street fight too with some idiots that don't even remember their names. And, what's more, if you punch them they risk falling on their stupid heads and maybe hitting concrete edges, involving serious complications. That was my reasoning and, as digesting it all we haven't responded, the idiots called us *Fucking Dagos* and kept rolling self-fulfilled down the street.

Kiro, having the long history of fights, drunk and sober, was always ready as a bull, just wave a red flag, but this time he carried his precious multi-clothes-hanger, and he was just passing by some drunken idiots looking not able enough to wipe their own ass.

I waited a couple of minutes and then told him what they said. He was so angry and wanted to go after them. The ironic thing is he's Macedonian and they mistook him for a Turk. It all becomes a farce. The idiots, the culture, the education... What are we fighting for in the end? Who is our enemy? Is it the color of the skin, or is it religion, or both?

We kept going, up the Kay Road, to our little house on the hill, only to get harassed by another *wild turkey,* this time Paul. No wonder why some people lose temper and smash everything. Only if you have a vision, a higher cause, you're above the ordinary madness…

————

A ruby sunrise… The sun is like a Red Texas Grapefruit.

I don't know why every red grapefruit I saw was from Texas.

Because I'm going back to the States, where all red grapefruits come from Texas? A change again, breaking of habits. Maybe it's the same old one, coming and going, coming and going away…

This time that's it. The immigration will give me *three compassionate months,* and then I'll come back to hang around here for a while, if I want to keep the residency.

When I went to talk to them a month ago, Oldwin told me it was on the Rocks, but it's been a couple of years they moved behind the Central Station. It's exactly where he headed to do some work, and I insisted to drop me off closer to the Rocks.

If I just followed *the path of least resistance,* as he called it, I would have gone with him straight to the spot. With my luck I think I would have still walked down to the Rocks only to discover the truth that I'm to walk all the way back. There's that something in me—*what is it?* Number 5, numerology, persistence, or is it just me being *German?* One often mistakes me for one.

With certain things I'm thorough, not stubborn, but more like a believer, following a given path. It's that others mostly give out wrong information. I follow like a soldier, taking it seriously. My friend George goes like a breeze, although he got stuck in the Suisse Alps in the end, actually, in the beginning.

After following the adventures around the world in our dreams, with a legendary blanket on the shoulder he went and stayed there now dealing with two wives and four kids.

I proceeded to the Merchant Marine. Again, I didn't just board the ship and go with the wind. I studied it first.

Now he dreams about finally starting to write seriously, while I've been doing it all along. No wives, no kids…

Face your fears, live your dreams, I can still remember writings on buses in Auckland, New Zealand, some ten years ago now. Ten here, ten there, slow learning, and things happen, like brand new days, piling up on a heap of joy and sorrow everywhere one goes, some face fears, some live in denial and can't face tomorrow…

George breaks away from the family forever, as his kids are lining up, and I'm forever breaking away from loneliness as the years go by…

Women don't care about those reasons. They know what they want, but somehow hardly get it in the end. What they get is grown up children and a man with broken dreams. And when they break his wings, or balls, it's like taking one of his lungs out. The other one he destroys smoking…

Pavo knows what he wants too. A ten year younger *nice little woman* to take care of his property, and, believe it or not, he'll find one, because *he doesn't want to put up with their bullshit, mate,* and that's it.

His divorce lasted nine long years and his wife's lawyers gave up.

They couldn't get blood out of the stone. And Pavo still builds…

His kids don't come visit, it's okay, *he gave them a house each.*

 Pavo doesn't put up with anybody's bullshit but his own…

Henry Miller said: *a writer needs to learn to live on his own.* He had five unsuccessful marriages and a few kids, and he was right. One can write alone only. One is to become a part of it and just flow. One can't do it surrounded by interfering vibes.

Now I can hear the sunrise, bird singing, clock ticking, occasional coughing and a car passing by, but if I heard a voice, just a word or a simple sentence, it would take my mind off.

When I go back to Portland, no way I can write. Maybe in some sudden stressed intervals when unexpectedly everyone disappears for a while, but by then, normally, one's mind is already shattered, and one is just to take deep breaths.

When they come back usually they throw a phrase in the air like a tennis ball, *go get it!*

A phrase goes something like: *what have you been doing all day?*

After a while they stop saying it and then there's only a certain configuration on their faces developed by strained inner forces. But you know what it means, because you can read their minds.

When they get used to *that,* then they expect you to do it all the time. And if you don't, they'll want you to do *something,* show some progress, give some results and, by the way, *what's wrong with your erection?*

Ask the doctor. He's supposed to have one too.

One of the last mornings in Kay Road 36…

I'm looking around this room bathed in sunshine and warmth, and in two days I'll be gone. In less than a month this old house will be erased giving room to a younger, better one. But this one now means much more, has a story built in, like a cabinet one uses to hide in and come out. The old deck around it like on a tramp steamer. One could *shoot* the sun every morning calculating its position, as it appears above the horizon, or just admire it…

When I remember first coming here, about a month ago, being terrified by the whole place, bugs and roaches, smelly feet, half-deaf Pavo telling his life story, remembering his father, childhood, boyhood, studying, marriage, Australia… I'm already missing it all.

Just now a little bug has crawled into the laptop and disappeared under the keys. It's either going to die inside the computer, or it'll crawl out in America and infest my mother's place.

It'll sure remind me of the bugs running across the walls and the table while Pavo chain-smoked, wiping them off as if they were crumbs of bread, focusing on telling his mesmerizing stories full of ancient wisdom and simplicity, ancient phrases that would take ages to translate. A simple folk's language that took centuries to grow.

You're going to drive around (meaning: *to fly) and leave me here like a bear in the cave,* said he this morning before going to work. He wants me to find him a nice woman to marry, someone to make him coffee and breakfast, wash and fold his clothes, and he'll bring his salary home...

I actually don't feel like leaving at all. This place has gotten under my skin. It's hard for me to write right now instead of just sitting on the deck and gazing adrift toward the Long Reef in bliss of detachment.

The sky is huge, crispy blue, the palms dance in the breeze, a dog barks in the distance, the washing machine purrs downstairs—a new, computerized model...

Everything just *is,* lots of space embraced with a sweep of the eye, and lots of time just to be. The carpets are old, hairy and orange, the clothes lie around unfolded, as if some ghosts tried them on overnight and then *left the building* in a hurry after enchanting houris...

The walls need painting, but the sunshine just pours in taking care of everything. I would never change it, never erase it. *It's perfect as is.* Maybe fix the deck a bit, all those nails that started coming out. It is amazing how the rest of the house is totally different feeling more like a cave Pavo referred to.

Downstairs is cold and humid, moldy as an underground world with the tenants like some sort of prisoners of their own device. The bathroom is falling apart, the walls are peeling off, but this room, as though it feeds off it, as if leaning on it all, is like the top of the world full of light, like a bridge of old Noah's Ark stuck on a hill after the flood is gone.

I could write here forever in this silence and this light, caressed by the palms and surrounded by big blue sky, while the rest of the world is filled with nonsense.

Even if I come back, it'll be a different place. This room will be gone. Who knows how the new one will feel like—like anything new, not broken in, walls of bricks, freshly painted and soulless, waiting on new stories to be walled in. Maybe the old ones won't fit…

There one goes again, nothing lasts forever. One can find a perfect spot and a perfect place, even hate it in the beginning, but one can hardly keep it. And one day, when one is finally able to get his own, it still will be impossible to get a perfect match like this. The rest of the house is horrible. It's there to keep this room in the air like a watchtower, with St. Sava, Njegoš, and a stuffed deer's head on the wall.

Just now I got a call from Miss E. from the immigration.

I was supposed to call her later on today. It's a really pleasant surprise that she is so responsible, correct and human. She didn't have to call me. It was my duty to find out her whereabouts, if I wanted my visa stamped.

Now she called again, and scared me a bit. I thought something went wrong because I started writing about her, but no, she just called to inform me that if I come today she won't be at the counter between 2 and 3.30. If all the clerks and officers were like her, this world would at least function better.

There goes a perfect example of me. I'm a sucker for kindness, honesty, genuine soul, human touch, what not. Miss E. had almost turned a sunny day into a nightmare yesterday.

I headed there with a song in my heart, bought a *day-tripper,* even the bus driver warmed up to the fact I paid $15 for it. Probably it's some kind of a bonus for them, like a daily score or something. He even asked me where I headed willing to help out if need be.

Unlike most of the drivers so far acting as if they were on a reserve rugby bench, or as if buses were their property, or as if they were some sort of drill sergeants. But before the bus ride, something nice happened. I went to the little family practice to get the copies of my blood test since Rachel reminded me in her email I better get all of it otherwise in the States I'd have to do it all over again. *In the States…*

So I got there just as Dr. G. was receiving a patient and quickly told him what I needed. A minute later he phoned the receptionist Mira. She then phoned the lab and the fax was on its way.

Do you need all results? (Meaning my Infertility test.)

No, I've got those. Not a problem, everything worked, smooth as.

After she handed them to me I told her I was going to see my family.

Oh, you're going to Bosnia?

No, they live in America now. Please tell the doctor I'll be back in a few months, because he was expecting to see me in a couple of weeks.

Not a problem, isn't he such a nice man?

Of course (I was a bit surprised by her genuinely open mind), I'm glad I happened to be his patient *(instead of that other guy,* biting my tongue).

Oh, I'm his patient too, and I feel so privileged to work for him, the world would be much better if there were more people like him.

And—like you too, I smiled walking out the door…

The rest of the waiting room was silent. It seemed like only Mira and I knew what we were talking about.

Thank you, she was flattered, *have a safe trip!*

Ms. E. was a different story.

On the phone she told me to look for her at the ground floor, counter number 10.

As I walked into a waiting room that could represent the U.N., she wasn't there. I normally shun the immigration because they had put me through a grinder. Every time I feel a bit uncomfortable having somebody browsing through my life and deciding about my destiny.

A week ago, Ms. E. told me to come next week, bring my birth certificate and she'd issue my visa. Since she wasn't there I went out to find a phone boot and call her.

At the same time I crossed the street and went to *TAFE* information to ask how to get to *Kogarah* and the Logistics Department and see about my Diploma from France.

People milled around, another beautiful day, girls showing off their long legs, some of them a bit too skinny, some too fat, but all following the latest fashion form *People Magazine*. Whatever Paris Hilton, Nicole Kidman, or Brittney Spears wear or do, they'll make sure to religiously follow it. Even if it looks ridiculous or senseless...

Ms. E. apologized she was in an emergency meeting, and already back at the counter 10. Again I didn't wait long enough. I thought while waiting one could do something *useful* too, but sometimes one is to just sit & wait.

After exchanging the forms of politeness, she asked me if I brought everything. I handed her my birth certificate: *it's all you told me to bring.*

She looked a bit puzzled but didn't say anything. She smiled politely with a little strain, excused herself and took my application to her supervisor. Then she came back browsing through the law manual, focusing on looking very professional and concerned.

It won't be a moment, she smiled and took off again. My smile was hanging in the air waiting encouraged by the previous conversation, phone calls, sunshine, Dr. G., Mira, even the bus driver...

It won't be a moment, no worries, *I've been waiting all my life,* I'll wait a few minutes longer, just be true.

But she had something about her, she was trying to be true a bit too hard. She said it was her first issuing of a 3-month visa, then she was just to put it in the computer, and for some reason she'd stop and take off again.

I believed, once more, but my gut was telling me something went on, something only immigration knows, their little tricks, nice and polite little questions just to, after all, tell you *sorry, something is wrong with the computer, and we normally don't issue these here, you better go up to the first floor and they'll do it for you…*

Is everything OK?

Oh, yes, not a problem, everything's fine!

She blushed, and I knew she lied, but I had no choice. I already got that butterfly feeling in my stomach. It's when you sense something they know and try not to tell you right away. They send you around to avoid the promises they made, passing them onto somebody else to *cut your had off.*

She organized the number for me, *H 355,* and I was up at the same counter *52,* where I talked to her one week ago, when after all the questions she said to come whenever to issue my visa.

My fault again—she was going to give it to me then, but it would mean one week less. It would be till July 24 instead of August 4, and I went with my old habit of sun chasing, getting as much summer in my life as possible. One can't have it all. The same old lesson never learned.

Same old counter, another woman… Completely different, a bit dreamy and soft, like a genuine nurse. Ms. E. gave me the phone number where they can reach her so she'd explain everything. But before it happened, I had to pretty much explain it myself, and since I was already put in that confusing limbo position, I did it a bit hastily and nervous.

When you have to repeat the same story a few times, it starts wearing off, becoming more and more unbelievable. The dreamy one didn't have her name displayed and she even seemed willing to give me a 5-year visa. Something I had already gave up on, although initially it was what I really needed.

The others before her gave me the impression it would be impossible to get it, considering my case. Haven't spent 2 out of 5 years here, and didn't have any proves to show I had ties with Australia. No wife, no job, no rental agreement…

And I still aimed at the impossible. But the dreamy one seemed willing to do it only if I showed anything, even just the proof that I rent the place, which I could have done, but it was too late, I leave in two days.

What's the point of getting a job and leaving it a few weeks later just to have a letter of employment? To the dreamy one that didn't seem to be an issue, and it made me feel a bit like being lead on again:

I could have done it if somebody had told me…

After seeing the letters about my father's illness, she asked an innocent question if I ever was back in Yugoslavia, and that innocent question turned everything around. I thought she was still thinking about maybe giving me 5 years, and I said yes, I did go there *briefly*, but that was a trap.

She went to her supervisor and brought me a big questionnaire to fill out. *When and where was I in Yugoslavia after 1991?* And was I the part of any military or paramilitary organizations?

I went only once on a special flight from Paris to pick up the death camps' refugees from the Zagreb airport and fly them back to France.

But how was I going to prove it? It was more than ten years ago, nobody ever asked me those questions.

The laws have changed. Obviously they looked for possible war criminals and I had no proof of my whereabouts from 1991 to 2000 on me. My old passport gone.

So I filled out the form, said that I was in the army, and that it was compulsory, 1983-1984, and that I lived in France since 1990.

It's OK, just put that.

But there was another part *B* where I was to give my officers' names, the places where military actions were taken, *et cetera*... How in the world could I remember it all, it was more than 20 years ago!

That was finally okayed too, I didn't have to put it. But I was on tenterhooks every time she'd send me to the waiting room, in her soft and dreamy way telling me that she'd come for me. And I waited and waited.

I didn't even know what they were doing, if they were questioning my whole residency again, digging about my history, last ten years spent in the air, flying between the continents, trying to do something with my music, writing, house-painting, landscaping, trying to be around my family, trying to be myself too, and in the end you end up in a waiting room where mainly women decide about your destiny. Maybe they're all connected with secret codes...

I went to the counter hesitating, because once in the American consulate they almost called the security just because I approached the without being called. She was still there, something soothing in her dreamy eyes, waiting for her supervisor's decision. The supervisor came too, apologetic, saying I could come tomorrow, while we all wait for answers...

But what is wrong?

They felt uncomfortable telling me they had to check my background and see if I committed any war crimes, *I* who escaped from it catching the last bus, *I* who worked with the refugees from the death camps, having nightmares from their stories...

They faxed my statutory declaration to Canberra, where I was being thoroughly checked. The main misunderstanding was when I said I went to Croatia once on that special flight from Paris. They thought I stayed there for awhile.

I had to explain now to the supervisor *and* the dreamy girl, again, that I was there only for a day, picking up those poor people gathered at the airport with yellow ribbons around their sleeves (other groups had different colors).

They were waiting to be shipped to a *Third Country*. It's another book I never finished. I was in a *Fourth Country* chasing ghosts…

Finally they had the approval from Canberra and I was getting the visa.

So, what if I hadn't mentioned that one trip to Zagreb?

She gave me her beautiful dreamy smile, *well, we wouldn't have checked then…*

I nearly bit my tongue off.

Again, I was put in that situation only because, once and for all, I didn't learn that *I've* been putting myself in it, because of the various reasons. But the reasons could have been reduced as well.

One could look up what tips stand for—to insure prompt service. It is where the apprehension of give-and-take as a mutual cooperation and understanding between people or groups lies, often involving concessions on all sides. It is a useful and beneficial exchange of ideas still requiring further working out…

While she waited for the visa to be printed out, I asked her how she got her job. She told me I could apply on the website. Very human and helpful. I asked her if I could come back to her. She already knew my case, reassuring me not to worry about it. *Everything will be okay!*

I asked for her name…

She said that *anybody could help me, as they always change the counters due to security measures…*

At the same time she wrote her name down adding:

You will be surprised when you see it…

It was a name from my country.

Life, at least mine, has sarcastic ways of spinning me around, always on the edge, bringing me to sanctuaries where I can take deep breaths, and so it goes, from one oasis to another until the desert in between them becomes just an endless sea.

I did ask for her a few months later, but they told me it was against their policy. We were from the same country and it could have suggested a possible set up...

ABOUT THE AUTHOR

Born in Sarajevo, lived in France, New Zealand, America, and Australia.
Following his teenage desire to *busk* his way around Europe, he winds up in Munich, Stuttgart, Aarhus, Amsterdam, Liege, Zurich, Lausanne...
When the war in his country broke out, he was studying in Paris.
In Laval, he worked with the ex-prisoners of the concentration camps in *Omarska* and *Manjača* liberated by the Red Cross.
After their integration, he joined his family in America.
He continued on to Australia, as far as the east is from the west...

Proof

Made in the USA
Charleston, SC
17 February 2013